THE TREE
NAMED JOHN

The University of North Carolina Press
Chapel Hill, N. C.

The Baker and Taylor Co.
New York

Oxford University Press
London

Maruzen-Kabushiki-Kaisha
Tokyo

"Pals"

THE TREE NAMED JOHN

BY JOHN B. SALE

With twenty-two Silhouettes
by JOSEPH CRANSTON JONES

CHAPEL HILL
THE UNIVERSITY OF NORTH CAROLINA PRESS
1929

First Printing August 1929
1500 Copies

Second Printing November 1929
2000 Copies

PRINTED IN THE UNITED STATES OF AMERICA BY
THE SEEMAN PRESS, DURHAM, NORTH CAROLINA

TO

MY MOTHER

PREFACE

In this book I have purposely dealt with the better and gentler side of the Negro—the only side that I knew in my boyhood, about thirty-five years ago, when I lived on a plantation near Columbus, Mississippi.

I have tried to avoid, and I hope successfully, the romantic glamour and the sentimentality that sometimes overcolor the Negro of those days. These sketches are realistic. Aunt Betsey and Uncle Alford—and the others—are "drawn from life." All of the incidents actually happened, and the superstitions were implicitly believed. While such superstitions among the Negroes are fast disappearing through the influence of education, and while many of the old beliefs have been lost, there still exists an almost unbelievable faith in certain signs and charms (see *Folk Beliefs of the Southern Negro,* by Newbell Niles Puckett), and the "cunjur doctor" thrives.

Of the older Negroes mentioned in this book, only Aunt Nervy is living, and she is over eighty.

Henry Porter, my playmate of long ago, is now a wanderer. He is of the nomadic type, like the memorable Negro in Dr. Odum's recent book, *Rainbow Round My Shoulder.* I have seen Henry only once in the past twenty years. Sam and Bird are still living on the plantation; and every time we meet, Sam reminds me, "Us is de same day's chillun." We were born on the same day.

The jail-house in "Ghos'es" is still standing, but of the tree that held the spike only the stump remains.

In "Spider-Bitten" the expression "Gawdlest" or "Gawdlested," used by Aunt Betsey, was possibly "Godless" at first. Here it is used as an oath, the only oath permitted church members (men or women) on pain of being called before the church body and publicly rebuked.

I wish to express my gratitude for valuable suggestions and stimulating encouragement to Dr. Newbell Niles Puckett, Assistant Professor of Sociology at Western Reserve University, to Dr. Howard W. Odum, Professor of Sociology at the University of North Carolina, to Mrs. L. G. Painter, of Columbus, Mississippi, and to Lawrence G. Painter, Professor of English at the Mississippi State College for Women.

John B. Sale

Columbus, Mississippi

CONTENTS

SPIRITS

THE TREE CASTS SHADOWS

THE TREE
NAMED JOHN

THE TREE

STRENGT'

The fire in the stove was beginning to burn brightly, water had been put on to heat, and above the din of pots and pans Aunt Betsey's voice was lifted in that joyous spiritual of promise:

> Ah got a right,
> You got a right,
> Us all got a right
> To de tree uv life.
> Po' mo'ner,
> You shell be free!
> Po' mo'ner,
> You shell be free!
> Po' mo'ner,
> You shell be free—
> W-h-e-n de good L-a-w-d set you free.

Grumbling, she left the kitchen and went to the pen where transplanted collard-stalks, sheltered from the cold winds of the north and west by a wall of brush and by planks overhead, still furnished greens for the table.

It was early in January, but already the winds tasted of spring. Aunt Betsey sniffed the air happily and examined the moss on the north side of an oak. "Hah! Ah knowed it, Lawd—yo' signs don't nevuh fail. When de shuck is thin on de corn en de moss is thin en stan' up, dat means short winter en early spring. Um sho is glad, too, 'ca'se mustid salid'll be hyere soon, en Gawd knows Um plum tiah'd uv nothin' but colluds en turnips en taters er maybe a sto'-bought cabbage—dey ain' no 'count," she said, turning to an imaginary companion, "you know dat. But," she continued in a tone of deep resignation, "Ah reggin dat somewhar in dis worl' dar's some folks whut ain' got dat much to eat, en us got t' thank Gawd fer dat." And she went sadly toward the kitchen.

Aunt Betsey was slightly above medium height, thin, with sharp features. Her skin held just enough of brown to escape being black. Her voice, so sweet in song, was tinged with a note of authority when she talked to the other servants. They paid her due reverence, for Aunt Betsey was an oracle. She knew everything there was to know, from wonderful tales of "ha'nts en hoodoos en witches" to what folks most liked to eat. She was a real personage in her sphere—the kitchen—and boasted that she had been "wid Ole Mis' en de fam'ly all my bawn days, en Ah ain' nevuh had to hit narry lick uv wuck in de fiel' les'n Ah wan' to, en dat sho wuz sildom." She considered field hands a lower order of being and always treated them with condescension and frequently with disdain. Among the servants the usual solution to a knotty problem was—"Ax Ai' Betsey. She knows." She was an authority on signs and omens and African materia medica. Her advice was sought by many, and her opinion carried weight.

Aunt Betsey was straight in spite of her fifty-five years and seventeen children, the oldest being but thirteen years her junior. Her head, always covered with a "haid-rag" of white cloth or a bright colored bandanna worn like a turban, was well poised on her shoulders, and her proud carriage gave color to her claim that her "grandaddy's daddy wuz a Affiken kang."

This morning she wore a bright gingham dress over numberless skirts. A blue-checked kitchen apron, already showing smut spots from the stove, fell from her shoulders to the floor. Around her neck she had tied a twisted string of red flannel. Suspended from this and hanging inside her dress was a red flannel bag that was itself a part of the charm it contained, worn against sickness and the malignant power of evil spirits. A wristlet and an anklet of the same material guarded her against rheumatism.

As soon as she was in the kitchen, "Ole Mistis" called from her room upstairs: "Betsey! Oh Betsey!"

"Hiesh!" She commanded the empty kitchen. "D'ju call me, Ole Mis'?"

"Yes, come here. I have something to tell you."

Aunt Betsey made a wipe or two at the offending spots on her apron and then took it off. "Ole Mis' is mighty 'tickler 'bout dirt en sich. Wunner howcome she ain' call me 'fo' Ah built dat fiah en got all smutted up?" she mumbled to herself. "White folks is jes lak dat."

Upstairs she stood by the fire until told to take a chair and listen. Ole Mis' took a letter from her workbasket and began to read. A family matter was to be discussed by the oldest members of the family—not by servant and mistress alone. Aunt Betsey listened with a frequent "Dar now!" "Bless Gawd!" "Do Jesus!" When the end was reached, she leaned back in the chair, and with hands tightly clasped in her lap she almost whispered, "Blessit Jesus an' de Lamb!" It was a prayer.

"Well, Betsey, what do you think of that?"

"Blessit be de Name, Ole Mis', whut kin us think uv it?
Did she say jes zac'ly when she gwi fin' it?"

"Just two months more, she said."

"En how she say she gittin' 'long, Ole Mis'?"

"Fine—just fine. Things couldn't be better."

"Ah mout ha' knowed dat, 'ca'se all day yistiddy Ah wuz
feelin' mighty low-sperrited 'bout nothin', en las' night Ah
dremp 'bout Miss Betty en woke up crynin'. Dem's two good
signs, Ole Mis', you know dat. Lemme git de almanac fer you,
Ole Mis', en you see how de moon gwi be den, please ma'm."

The expected time was found to be shortly before, or in the
first few days following, the new moon. "Jes right, Ole Mis',
jes right. Dat's be bes' time fer birthin' chillun, 'ca'se de moon's
gedderin' strengt' t' come new, en de baby is gittin' strengt' t'
come wid it. En ef it come jes atter de new moon, dat's jes ez
good, 'ca'se de Bible say 'ez de moon wax strong in de heb'm,
so will de young on de ye'th.' You know dat. Do you reggin
you could fin' dat place in de Bible en read hit t' me right
now, Ole Mis'?"

"I am afraid I can't find that—not right now anyway," she
answered smiling. Betsey was much given to misquotations—
and worse.

"You's gwi write t'er dis week, ain't you?"

"Yes indeed, probably today."

"Well, den, when you do, Ole Mis', be sho t' tell 'er not t'
be skeered 'ca'se d'ain' nothin' t' be skeered uv—jes take kyere
uv herse'f, en eve'y day bathe her lines [loins] wid dishwatter,
en don' let nothin'—no cat er dawg er rat er snake ner nothin'
—skeer 'er, 'ca'se dat'll mark de baby. En tell 'er, Ole Mis', she
ought t' drink milkweed tea reg'lar, t' make de breas'-milk
strong, en ef she put some mullein in it, dat'll he'p. (Great
Gawd! But dar's a heap dat chile don' know, ain' dey?) En
anudder thing, Ole Mis', tell 'er t' be *sho* t' tie a red flannin

straing roun' 'er wais' fer strengt'. Be sho t' tell 'er dat. W'en us gwine up dar?"

Ole Mis' didn't know—not right away at any rate. Besides, for the present at least, she thought the doctors up there would look after her all right.

"Ye'm, Ah spec' dey'll do de bes' dey kin, but dey don' know hit all, Ole Mis', you know dat. Us'll sho ha' t' go 'fo' long. M-y Gawd'lmighty!" she burst out, "Hyere Um is talkin', en Ah bet my fiah's plum out in de stove, en dem colluds ain't on." At the door she said, "Be sho t' tell 'er whut Ah said, Ole Mis', en tell 'er us gwi be dar soon."

After Aunt Betsey rekindled the fire in the kitchen and put the collards in the pot, she gave herself up to reverie: "Jes yistiddy, seems lak—jes yistiddy. Lawd Gawd, Ah mus' be gittin' ole. 'Twa'n't no longer ago 'n yistiddy, seems lak, she wuz a baby, en me a-nussin' her. Now she gwi ha' a baby herse'f— Lawd, Lawd, Lawd! Miss Betty ought t' come home whar me en Ole Mis' could look atter her. Sho ought t' do dat, now. Doctors—huh! Dey good sometimes but dey don' know hit *all*, dat dey don't. Ef dey wuz de onliest ones whut know anything, a heap a folks whut livin' now 'ud be daid en gone t' glory er somewhar ilse, 'ca'se dar wouldn' be enough doctors t' go roun', dat dar wouldn'. Doctors say fus' dis en den dat don' do no good. Doctors—huh! Ah done had seb'mteen chillun, Ah is, en ain' los' but one in de birthin', en de moon wuz wrong den. But de moon gwi be right dis time, thank Gawd, en whut wid dat, en de udder things Um gwi do m'se'f, dat chile sho gwi have a good start."

As soon as dinner was on and could be left in safety for a few minutes, Aunt Betsey went upstairs again. "Ole Mistis," she asked as soon as she entered the room, "Is you writ dat letter yit?" No, the letter had not been written. "Um's glad uv dat—sho, 'ca'se dar's one thing Ah fergot t' tell you t' tell Miss Betty en dat's dis: Tell 'er, please ma'am, fer Gawd's sake be

kyereful en don' cross no runnin' watter. Dat's de dange'usest
thing she could do right now. En ef she jes ha' t' do it, tell 'er
fer t' be sho t' shet her eyes tight 'fo' she start 'cross en t' keep
'em shet atter she over de bridge twel she count nine en den
make a cross mark in de road en spit in it. But you tell her de
bes' thing is not t' cross it. You know dat's so, don'chu, Ole
Mis'?"

"Well, Betsey, I've heard that all my life, and I know
lots of folks believe it. So I'll tell her that for you, too," said
Ole Mistis, smiling.

"Yes'm, dey do, Ole Mis', dey sho do b'lieve it, 'ca'se hit's
Gawd's trufe. Lawd," she exclaimed suddenly, "Ah got t' run
ag'in! Mars John'll be hyere terreckly, holl'in' lak all gitout
'ca'se dinner's late."

Uncle Alford came into the kitchen before the servants had
finished their dinner. "Sis Betsey," he said, "Mars John tole me
Ah could git some dinner t'day, dat is, ef you had any to spar',
please ma'm. De ole lady is sorta po'ly-lak at home en ain' fix
nothin' much to eat. En 'sides dat, sick er well, her cookin' don'
tas'e lak yo'n do, nohow, en dat's a fac'."

Uncle Alford was one of the tenants on the place, but for
years he had shined Mars John's shoes every morning, and on
Sundays he drove the carriage. This, in Aunt Betsey's estima-
tion, put him on a higher level than that of the ordinary field
hands on whom she looked down. To use her own words,
"He been hyere so long now, twel he mos' house-broke."

Aunt Betsey smiled. "Come in, Brer Alfo'd, us got plenty.
Put yo' cheer t' de table en set down." She put food within his
reach, poured his coffee, and then brought out a quarter-section
of dried-peach pie. She was proud of her cooking, and Uncle
Alford knew that flattery was the surest road to the enjoyment
of it. Presently she said, "De's sump'm Ah wants you t' do
fer me, Brer Alfo'd, en Ah wants you t' do it right off. Ah
wants you t' put a aige on a knife fer me. Ah don' mean no

brick-bat aige, needer. Ah could do dat m'se'f. Ah wants a smooth aige whut'll cut, en cut smooth en easy, en Ah wants you t' fix hit right off fer me. Is you gwi do it?"

"Sho, Sis Betsey, sho. When you wan' it?"

"Right off—jes ez soon ez you kin do it."

"Well," he said hesitatingly, "Ah don' spec' Ah kin fix it fer you dis dinner time 'ca'se Ah—"

Aunt Betsey reached over his shoulder, picked up the pie, and handed it to the house-girl. "Hyere, Net," she said, "put dishyere in de safe, gal, peach pie's too skase to be handin' hit roun' permisc'us."

Uncle Alford looked hurt. "Ez Ah wuz sayin', Sis Betsey, Ah cain't do it dis dinner time *onlest* you lemme take hit home to whar Ah kin git t' my *good* whet-rock. Dat's whut Ah wuz sayin', Sis Betsey."

"O-o-h, hit 'twuz, 'twuzzit? En when is Um gwi git dat knife back?"

"E-er—well, Ah'll ha' plenty a time t' sharp'm hit good twixt now en bell time. Ah'll fetch it by yo' house den." With a feigned air of misgiving she put the pie by him again, and by it she laid a bone-handled case knife. Smiling, she said to Net, "Take sump'm 'way f'um dey belly en you kin make 'em do mos' anything. Mens is jes lak dat." Uncle Alford heard but said nothing; his mouth was full of pie.

When the dishes were washed and the kitchen was closed until time to prepare supper, she went back to see Ole Mistis. "Ole Mis'," she said, "Didn' Ah see some uv Miss Betty's ole clo's hangin' up in de closet de udder day? Um piecing a quilt, en Ah wants t' git some white cloth jes lak whut Ah seed, please ma'm." She got it, and when she left, Ole Mis' smiled gently, wondering to herself just what Aunt Betsey was up to.

Aunt Betsey was up to a plenty. Uncle Alford brought her the knife just as she reached home. She put Miss Betty's dress that Ole Mis' had given her into one corner of her bureau drawer and the knife into another corner. She hesitated a moment before closing it. Then she took the knife out and put it into her clothes chest. "Mustn't let 'em git too clost yit aw'ile—mout start cuttin' too soon, en 'sides dat, Um got some thinkin' t' do. Now lemme see," she pondered, "A sharp knife cuts de birthin' pains quick, but hit lets 'em bleed too much. Now how's Um gwi git roun' dat? A dull, rusty knife don' bleed 'em so much, but Lawd—how hit do hurt in de cuttin'. Ah knows, Ah does, 'ca'se Ah done 'spe'enced bofe uv 'em. Dar's jes' nach'ly boun' t' be some way uv gittin' roun' dis, dough. Dat chile's pain got t' be cut quick, en Um got t' save de bleedin' too. Lawd," she said, looking upward, "You knows dar is a way t' do dis, en Ah knows hit, too, en Um astin' you right now t' he'p me. Do Jesus, show me de way." She sat for a moment with her eyes closed, and then—"Hit'll come soon," she said and left the house. Nearly all of the young women were in the fields knocking cotton stalks down with long sticks so that the plows could cover them easily. On her way through the quarters she stopped once or twice to talk to some of the older women, refusing to tarry with them long, however. She was going to the woods to get some wild cherry bark to make some tea and for some other things. "Tea?" asked one, laughingly, "Ah didn' know womens ez ole ez whut you is, needed no wile cherry bark tea. Is it fer yo'se'f, Sis Betsey?" asked one.

"Naw, honey," she replied, "hit ain' fer me 'ca'se Ah done been off de waggin fer de rise uv ten yeah now, *but,* ez fer who hit *is* fer—dat ain' none uv yo' business."

In the woods she found the wild cherry tree and cut a quantity of the bark from the north side—the strong side. "En dat's dat," she said aloud. "Now fer de name-tree. Hit's got t' be a good un, too." She wanted a "soon budder." A hackberry buds first of all, but its bark is too rough. A baby with a rough-barked name-tree like that was apt to grow up mean-tempered.

"Presently she found a straight elm sapling"

She considered a straight oak sapling, but oaks were the last trees to bud. "A oak fer strengt'. Dat baby is gwine t' need strengt' too, but a oak is sich a late budder, en hit grow so slow." Presently she found a straight elm sapling that was about the height of her shoulder. The tiny points of the buds looked as if they were just waiting for half a chance to thrust themselves out. She smiled happily as she examined it—every twig was healthy. "Dat's de one," she said, "quick budder, grows fas', en, Lawd, how tough a ellum is! Tree," she went on, "you ain' gwi be hyere fer long now. Jes ez soon's dat baby's bawn Um gwi move you up to my house whar Ah kin watch you. En when Ah plants you Um gwi name you fer dat baby, en Ah tells you *right now,* Ah wants you t' grow en grow good." She tied a large piece of white cloth on it so that it could be found easily and then went back to the quarters— one problem still unsolved. "Dat bleedin'—Ah knows dar is a way t' stop it—jes boun' t' be a way ef Ah could only think uv it. Maybe Ah kin dream it t'night."

THE NAME-TREE

In the month that followed, Aunt Betsey spent many happy, thoughtful hours. The day after the name-tree was selected she wrapped the knife in the dress and put them away in her "clo's chis'"; later she would wrap them in red flannel to give them strength, but it was too soon for that now. "Ef she wuz at home now, a mont' 'fo' de time 'ud be soon enough," she said, talking to herself, "but ez she so fur away, hit ain' no harm t' start now 'ca'se hit take hit so long fer de good uv hit t' reach 'er." At the end of the month, though, she would put the knife and dress under the bed and two weeks later would wrap the red flannel around them. "Den dey start wuckin', sho 'nough."

Only one thing happened to disturb her thoughts. Toward the last of the month, while she was in her cabin smoking her after-dinner pipe, a house wren lit on her doorsill. "Hiesh!" she whispered to herself. "Lawd," she prayed, "don' let it come no fudder—dat's bad 'nough ez 'tis." She sat motionless, watching every movement the bird made. Little Miss Wren was undecided what to do. As if aware of the anxiety she was causing and wanting to prolong it, she tipped from one end of the sill to the other and looked into the semidarkness of the room uncertainly, then—wheeled and flew away. "Now whut do dat means? Hope t' Gawd she tuck de bad luck wid 'er," said the old woman. She got some sulphur and scattered a little over the doorsill to drive the bad luck away, but she was doubtful that it could be done. "Anyhow, hit could ha' been wuss," she said, "'ca'se ef she had a come in, hit would a meant death, but ez 'tis, she jes fotch bad luck uv some kin', en Ah sho hope she ain' lef' it. Gawd!" she exclaimed with a shudder, "jes sposen Ah had a move en skeered 'er into drappin' dat bad luck 'fo' she flew off, er wuss still, made 'er come fetch hit in de house! Dat 'ud been bad, sho 'nough."

Her happy disposition soon responded to the warm sunshine of approaching spring; rarely did gloom sit on her shoulders long. There were three hours "er sich a matter 'fo' time t' start supper," and she decided to spend the time visiting "Sis Nervy," a crony of hers, a fellow member of "de I John Baptis' Chu'ch en one uv my Sisters in Chris'." Minerva lived at the other end of the quarters some distance away.

Long before Aunt Betsey reached there she heard coming from the house the sound of heavy blows and a wailing voice promising—"Ah ain' gwi do it no mo', mammy. Thanky ma'm—thanky ma'm, mammy, thanky ma'm. Ah ain' do it no mo'."

Then came the voice of Sis Nervy, high pitched in righteous anger: "Ah *t-e-l-l-s* you not t' do dat 'ca'se hit's bad luck, en you don' pay me no min'. Jes say dey *ain'* no sich thing en keep a-comin', you sassy devul! *'Ny-in'* luck en 'sputin' me, too. *Shet up* dat crynin'," she snapped savagely, "en go fetch me a bucket uv water en thank yo' Gawd dat dat rope wa'n't wet, er Ah'd a cut yo' clo's off'n you wid it, you nappy-haided, blue-gummed heifer! *Git!*"

Aunt Betsey met the whimpering girl at the gate and smiled in sympathy; she knew Sis Nervy's hand was heavy. Inside the gate she stumbled over the handle of a hoe left lying across the walk. "My Gawd! D'ju ever see sich kyerelessness ez dat?" she exclaimed. She hastily stepped over it backwards and made a cross mark on the ground. Then she picked the hoe up and leaned it against the fence.

"You is mighty kyereless wid yo' hoes en things, Sis Nervy," she said, entering the house. Then—"Good e'nin', Sis Nervy, is you well?" Politeness demanded this salutation, however late.

Sis Nervy was still angry. "Hit wuz dat no-mannered, uppity gal done dat. Good e'nin', Sis Betsey. Jes 'fo' you come Ah tole her t' git de spade en dig up dat patch uv nut grass in de gyarden, en w'en Ah look up, hyere she come th'ough de house wid dat hoe en *hit on her shoulder*. En w'en Ah tole her she knowed dat wuz de wuss kin' uv bad luck, en fer her t' go back, she jes keep a-comin', she did, en try t' laugh en say dar ain' no sich thing. En w'en Ah ax her who say dat, she up en say 'Mister Gum.' Den Ah tuck dat well-rope en Ah *prove* hit t'er, Ah did, dat hit *wuz* bad luck. Ef dat 'Mister Gum' nigger is gwine quit l'arnin' 'em books en tries to l'arn 'em dat whut us knows is so *ain'* so, den Ah ain' gwi let her go t' dat school no mo'."

"You's right, Sis Nervy, you sho is right 'bout dat, en a well-rope is de bes' thing dar is t' make em l'arn quick. You know de Bible say 'Spare de rod en spile de chile,' en dat's de trufe."

"Hit sho is, Sis Betsey, hit sho is, en ef de Lawd spares me, ain' none uv mine gwi be spiled dat way. But how is you been gittin' 'long, Sis Betsey, is you been well?"

"Jes sorta so-so, Sis Nervy, Ah had a tech uv mis'ry in my back de fus' uv de week en hit ain' plum lef' me yit." For nearly an hour they talked of their ailments and those of their friends far and near, and then they talked of religion. They were in the midst of analyzing the differences between "baptizing" Baptists and "sprinkling" Methodists when they were interrupted by Net's voice calling Aunt Betsey.

"Whutchu want, gal?"

"Come t' de house, quick. Ole Mistis want you."

Aunt Betsey left hurriedly, promising to come back if she could. At the house Net refused to tell her what Ole Mistis wanted, but she was smiling.

Upstairs Ole Mistis told her the news. A telegram, just brought, said the baby, a boy, had arrived and all were well.

For a moment the old woman was stunned, but not for long. "Blessit Lawd en Savior *en* Hallelooyer too, Ole Mis'. Glory to Gawd A-*man!* Whutchu reggin dey gwi name it?"

"Oh I've known all along that if it was a boy it would be named for his Uncle John."

Said Aunt Betsey solemnly, " 'His name is John.' Dat's a good name, Ole Mis'. 'Ceptin' uv Jesus's hit's de bes' in de Bible. But you look hyere, Ole Mis'," she exclaimed horror-stricken, "Hit come too soon! M-y G-a-w-d! De moon ain' right; hit's wanin' hard! Wunner how cum she fin' hit now?"

Ole Mistis tried to allay her fears but to no avail. She excused herself presently to start supper, she said, but she stopped at the kitchen only long enough to tell Net to light the fire for her if she didn't get back in time. Supper must not be late, but there was something she just had to do right off. She started to her house, mumbling all the while, "Wunner ef dat knife started cuttin' too soon, Lawd? Umph, umph, umph.

How come it, Lawd, how come it? Ah betchu dat fool Alfo'd nigger made dat knife too sharp. Dat mus' be de matter, en ef hit is, he kin starve t' death 'fo' he eats anudder mou'ful in my kitchen, de no-sense-ed ole fool. Co'se Ah didn' wan' de knife dat sharp—anybody 'ud know dat. But you cain' tell a ole fool nigger man nothin'—dey knows hit all, dey do."

She separated the knife and dress with almost frantic haste, and to the knife she said, "Ef you is de ca'sen uv dis, Um sho gwi spile yo' aige 'g'inst a brickbat en th'ow you away fer good en all."

She went to Minerva's house and found her making ready to cook supper. "Let dat gal do it, Sis Nervy, en len' me yo' spade en you come on wid me, too. Miss Betty done foun' dat baby, hit's a boy en name fer Mars John, en de moon's all wrong fer it, hit is. Wunner how come she couldn' waited a week anyhow?"

"Lawd, Sis Betsey," exclaimed Sis Nervy, "you don' tell me! I-s she? When?"

"Dis mo'nin' er las' night er yistiddy, don' jes zac'ly know which. Whar dat spade?"

Sis Nervy got the spade from the "gyarden." "Now whut us gwi do?" she asked.

"Gwi git dat baby's name-tree en set hit out. Ah would ha' tole you 'bout hit 'fo' dis but hit's bad luck to talk 'bout hit too soon, hit is, you know dat." And the two old women left on a labor of love.

The tree having been brought to Aunt Betsey's garden and the hole dug, she asked, "Sis Nervy, whut you reggin would be de bes'; de sun mos' down now, en weak'nin'. Would you plant hit now er wait twel jes 'fo sunup en ketch de strengt' uv de risin' sun?"

"Ah b'lieve Ah'd wait."

"You gwi he'p me in de mo'nin' den, soon?"

"Sho, Sis Betsey, sho. Jes ez soon ez Mars John wakes de folkses you be ready en Ah'll come en us'll do it."

"Dat's all *right* den. But don' talk, hyeah me? Don' talk, hit's bad luck t' do dat 'fo' us gits it planted."

Uncle Alford came by the kitchen for his supper that night and was pained into silence when his pleasantries were met with—"Ah ain' got no time t' was'e on a fool." He never learned why she said that.

Mars John never used a bell to wake the hands in the morning; he called each one by name. His voice, loud and clear as a bugle, would rise over the tree tops—"H-e-y, J-o-h-n Lewis," "H-e-y, A-l-fred," and would in turn be answered from the cabins—"Y-e-s s-u-h!" The day's work would have begun.

Almost at Mars John's first call there was a tap on Aunt Betsey's door and a low voice called, "Sis Betsey!"

"Datchu, Sis Nervy?"

"Yessum. 'S you ready?"

"Comin' right now."

In the garden one held the tree while the other shoveled in the dirt and packed it. No word was spoken until this was done.

"Ah wush hit had been so Ah could a wattered it wid de baby's fus' bathin' watter," meditated Aunt Betsey. "Dat 'ud made 'em blood kin, plum en sho. You know dat, Sis Nervy."

Then Sis Nervy asked, "Is us gwi sing dat plantin' song?"

"Dat's a moon song, Sis Nervy, d' you reggin hit 'ud be right t' do dat?"

"Well, us kin change it f'um 'moon' to 'sun' en sing it. 'Twon' do no harm nohow, en hit looks better anyways."

"Well, aw right, den. You sing it en Ah'll gi' de 'sponses en bofe uv us come in on de A-man."

Both faced the east and Sis Nervy began:

                    "New sun, Sister."
                      "Yes, Lawd."
                    "New life, Sister."
                      "Yes, Lawd."
                    "Shine on sun."
                      "Yes, Lawd."
                    "Grow on, tree."
                      "Yes, Lawd."
                    "He'p 'em, Jesus,"
                      "A-a-man."

The tree was planted.

AUNT BETSEY TAKES CHARGE

Little John was nearly a year old before Aunt Betsey saw
him, although "Ole Mistis" had been to see him several times.
Since his coming he had never been strong, and now he was
cutting his teeth. Aunt Betsey made anxious inquiry every
time the mail came: "Is aire letter come f'um Miss Betty?"
and, "How she say dat chile gittin' 'long?" When the little
fellow was at his worst and the whole family in despair, Aunt
Betsey was sympathetic. It hurt her heart to think of "dat chile
suff'rin' lak dat en all on account uv—whut?" she asked herself angrily. She had feared at first that she was partly to
blame. She might have miscalculated, but she cast that fear
aside and placed the blame where it belonged—on Uncle
Alford. He had "made dat knife too sharp. He de ca'sen uv it.
Ah gits mad eve'y time he come in my kitchen, Ah does, en
w'en Ah sees 'im settin' up to dat table, eatin' us vittles en
lickin' 'is chops en grinnin' fer all de worl', jes lak a tormcat
whut jes cotch a rat, Ah mos' pops. De ole fool!" She was
sympathetic, but unworried. She knew things. Every day she
visited the name-tree. No grass or weeds were allowed to

grow within the reaches of its midday shadow. "Dey ain' narry dead leaf on it," she would tell Sis Nervy. "He gwi be all right atter w'ile. Ah wushes to Gawd, dough, Miss Betty'd fetch 'im on home whar Ah could look atter 'im fer a w'ile, anyhow. She young, Sis Nervy," she went on, "en dar's a heap a things she don' know 'bout chilluns yit, whilest me, Ah done had seb'mteen, Ah is, en Ah done fergit mo' 'bout raisin' chillun den whut mos' folks ever *is* know. You know dat's de trufe, don'chu?"

Sis Nervy agreed with her. "Ain' many folks had de 'spe'ence like whut you is, Sis Betsey. Ah 'members mighty well, Ah does," she went on, "dat w'en my baby gal wuz sick wid de colic, nobody ner nothin' didn' do her no good 'ntwel you made dat chicken gizzard-linin' tea en gi'n 'er. She got well right off, she did, en she been a healthy chile f'um dat day 'ntwel now, she sho is. But 'bout dat chile uv Miss Betty's, how's hit gittin' 'long? Is you hyearn lately?"

"Hit ain' been doin' so well, Sis Nervy," Aunt Betsey answered. "Ole Mis' got a letter yistiddy whut said hit done started teethin', en 'is mouf wuz mighty so'e. Ah biled de meat off'n sum chaneybeh'ies en made a necklis fer 'im las' night, en Ole Mis' say she gwi sen' it t'er en tell 'er Ah say to let dat chile w'ar it. Dat'll he'p, 'ca'se dey's good fer dat, but de bes' uv all dar ain' no use tellin' 'er 'bout, 'ca'se Ah know she ain' gwi do it."

"Whut dat she ain' gwi do?" asked Nervy.

"H-a-a-h L-a-w-d," Aunt Betsey laughed exultantly, "dey's a heap a things she ain' gwi do dat's gwi be did anyways, 'ca'se," she lowered her voice to almost a whisper, "'ca'se Ah's done done it."

"*You is?*" Astonishment spread all over Sis Nervy's face, "How you—whutchu done?"

But Aunt Betsey wasn't ready to tell just yet. "Now, Sis Nervy, she said, "dar's a heap a things whut's good fer teeth-

ers, you know dat, en some uv 'em is better den de udders—
dat's a sho thing."

"Dat's de trufe, Sis Betsey, dat's de trufe, *sho*," agreed Sis
Nervy.

"Well," continued the old woman, "dar is, fus'," she held
up her hand and began to mark off on her fingers, "dar is,
fus', de chaneybeh'ies. Den come de hawg-teeth necklis. Dey's
good, 'ca'se a hawg's teethes is strong en sharp, en a necklis
made out'n dem will sho he'p cut th'ough dem gums en make
de teethes come quick. Den," she counted on, "dar's de rabbit
skin—de belly skin uv a boa' rabbit fer a boy baby er ilse a
sow rabbit fer a gal baby. Now some folks sez twis' it in a
straing en tie hit roun' de baby's wais'; but Ah sez, tie hit
roun' hit's nake, 'ca'se de teethes is clos'ter to 'is nake den dey
is to 'is wais', en de clos'ter to dem teethes hit gits de mo' he'p
hit gwi be. Dat's reason'ble, ain't it?' Nervy agreed to this also.

"Dar's a heap mo' things Ah could name, but Ah won't, like
rabbit brains, er elderbeh'ies, er buttons, er snake rattles, er
nutmegs en a heap a things, en dey's good, too, dey is; but de
bes' one uv all uv 'em is dis. Take a fiel' mouse (dey's de bes')
en run a needle en white thread th'ough one eye en out de
udder'n, en, w'ile hit's still kickin', hang it roun' de baby's
nake next t' de skin en let hit hang dar. *Dat's* de bestes' uv all."

Sis Nervy nodded in confirmation; she knew this was a good
remedy—one of the best—but what she didn't know was:
Why hang the mouse on the baby's neck before it was dead?
All the old folks said do that, she knew, but why?

"Dat's easy, Sis Nervy," explained the old woman, "Ah kin
show you dat jes ez plain ez day. Life fer life en strengt' fer
strengt'; hit's jes lak dat all over de worl', you know dat. So,
ez de life leave de mouse, hit goes into de baby en peartens up
dem teethes en gives de baby strengt' to stan' it; en, 'fo' Gawd,
Sis Nervy, dat baby'll ha' eve'y one uv 'is teethes 'fo' hit know
hit's been teethin'."

Sis Nervy was deeply impressed. "Dat's reason'ble enough," she admitted, "hit sho is. But whut wuz dat you done done?" she asked again.

"Hah! Lawd," Aunt Betsey laughed triumphantly, "Ah done fix it! You come en see."

At her house she led Aunt Nervy to the garden where together they had planted the name-tree. "See dat?" she asked, pointing. From its biggest limb and close to its little trunk hung a mouse. Bloody white thread through the eyes held it in place. "Hit 'ud been better, uv co'se, ef Ah could hung hit roun' dat baby's nake," she mused, "but dis'll be jes ez well, Ah spec', 'ca'se Ah kin let it hang hyere twel hit drap off, en Ah couldn' do dat wid de baby."

"Sis Betsey," Sis Nervy's voice was low and solemn, and her eyes spoke volumes of praise, "ef Ah had de sense whut you is got, Sis Betsey, ef Ah knowed whut *you* knows, Ah'd *do* things."

"Well, Sis Nervy," the old woman answered as she expanded under this praise, "Ah could do things, uv co'se; but sence Ah done got 'ligion en Jesus wash my sins away en de Lawd save me, Ah ain' done no cunjerin' a-tall 'ceptin' fer good. Ah could, dough, ef Ah jes would. You know dat."

During almost two months, except for more encouraging reports of the baby, everything went on as usual. The cheerful news was no surprise to Aunt Betsey, of course; she expected it. The name-tree was strong and healthy, and the mouse, dried to skin and bones by the hot suns of late fall, still hung from its branches, swaying gently back and forth with every breeze against its trunk. Of course that baby was all right. Didn't all the signs point that way? Hadn't she had good dreams about that baby for the last three Friday nights "han' runnin'," and hadn't she told those dreams before breakfast, before she had taken a mouthful of anything, even water? That was a good sign, everybody knew that, of course, they did. She had long talks with Ole Mis' every day and recounted to her all these signs. She didn't tell her about the mouse, Ole Mis' mightn't like that; and, besides, "nobody but a fool'll tell *eve'y* thing dey do, anyhow."

A few days more and Miss Betty wrote that the baby was so much improved that she was going to make the long delayed visit home. Aunt Betsey listened with beaming face. "Ah knowed it, Ole Mis'," she interrupted excitedly, "Ah knowed it. 'Tain't no news t' me, Ole Mis', 'ca'se yistiddy e'nin' w'en Ah shet up de kitchen atter Ah got th'ough wid de dinner dishes, a bluebird flew up in de chaneybeh'y tree by de dairy en lit, hit did, en look twoge de house. Ah knowed right den dey wuz comin' soon! Whut day she say dey's comin'?"

"Betsey," laughed Ole Mis', "let me finish, *please*. They are coming tomorrow!"

"Now bless de Lawd," the old woman said softly, "At las'!" Soon she aroused herself with a jump. "Great Gawd," she exclaimed happily, "de cookin' us got t' do! Miss Sallie gwi make pies en cakes en sich dis e'nin', Ah know, en Um gwine t' see 'er 'bout dat right off. Us is got a good late gyarden, Ole Mis', thank Gawd fer dat, en, 'sides, us is got taters en I'sh taters en punkins en dried okry fer soup en dried peaches en fus' dis en den dat en de udder en Gawd knows whut all." She caught her breath and continued, "Well, Um's gwine now en he'p Miss Sallie git dem cakes en things out'n de way, 'ca'se, me—t'morrow Ah's gwine to *spread* myself."

At the door she paused long enough to say, "Ole Mis', no sooner 'en you tole me dey 'uz comin', Ah knowed hit 'uz gwi be t'morrow, 'ca'se dat bluebird set in dat tree en pick 'is fedders lak he 'uz gittin' ready fer sump'm in a huh'y, en Ah knowed hit 'uz dat. You 'members Ah tole you so, didn' Ah?" And she was gone, leaving Ole Mis' laughing at the empty doorway.

Uncle Alford was in the kitchen for dinner the next day—
he was to drive the carriage to the train, and, for the first time
in many months, Aunt Betsey treated him as of old. After
more than one generous helping he began to expand—liter-
ally, and, encouraged by the warmth of her smile, he ventured
a compliment. "Lawd, Sis Betsey," he said, wiping his mouth
on his sleeve, "whut a cook you is!"

"D'ain' nothin' mo' hyere fer you, Brer Alfo'd," she snapped.

"Don' want no mo', Sis Betsey. Um 'bout t' bus' ez hit is.
Whut make you say dat?"

"'Ca'se you allus say dat en den hol' out yo' han' fer mo'.
Ah knows you, nigger," she laughed at him, "you knows Ah
does."

Uncle Alford chuckled appreciatively, "Ah cain' 'spute 'g'inst
you, Sis Betsey, 'ca'se you is mos' allus right. But *dis* time,
even ef you wuz t' gi' me dat li'l piece uv tater pie," looking
at it longingly, "Ah don' b'lieve Ah could—Ah ain' sayin' Ah
wouldn' try, now—but Ah don' b'lieve Ah could swollit," he
ended dismally.

Aunt Betsey looked at him jeeringly, "Ah knowed it! Ah
knowed you couldn' no mo' keep f'um axin' fer it den you
could keep f'um eatin' it ef you knowed hit 'uz gwi bus' you
wide op'm! Hyere, nigger, eat it—eat it en *bus'!*"

When it was nearly time for the carriage to be hitched, she
asked the old man if he was going to drive the mules he
worked himself; they were quiet and steady.

"Mules?" he asked, surprised, "No'm, Um's drivin' dem
hosses."

"Whutchu mean? Dem skittish hosses?"

"Dey ain' skittish, Sis Betsey, jes lively lak dey orter be,
whut wid de feedin' dey gits."

"Brer Alfo'd, you know better'n dat," Aunt Betsey said positively. "Dem hosses is downright skittish—not t' say skeery—
en hyere you is gwine hitch em up en go fer dat baby en Miss

Betty. You ain' got no sense! Sposen dat baby gits skeered de fus' time hit comes home? Dat 'ud make a rovin' man out uv im, en you know it. He never would stay at home. Den ag'in, sposen Miss Betty git skeered en spile 'er milk en gi' dat chile mo' colic den whut he already got? *Naw,* you jes wan' t' drive dem prancin' hosses, en, lak de fool you is, you ain' thought uv nothin' ilse. You's gwine to drive *mules,* nigger."

"Ah ain't!" he said indignantly.

"You is!"

"But, Sis Betsey, Mars John done said to—"

"You wait right hyere. Um gwine dis minute en talk to Miss Sallie en Ole Mis' en see whut *dey* say." At the door she turned for a parting shot: "Ef you leaves hyere t' ketch dem hosses 'fo' Ah gits back, de vittles you gits out'n dis kitchen f'um dis time on won' keep a chicken alive, much less bus' no buttons off yo' britches," she said, calling attention to the button he had unfastened at dinner time.

Miss Sallie and Ole Mis' listened, and Uncle Alford drove—mules.

It was pitch dark when the carriage returned from the station; the train had been late. Aunt Betsey, with the rest of the family, crowded around the carriage; and before anyone had alighted—before they had even been seen—her voice rose in noisy welcome: "Howdy, Miss Betty, how you do? Gawd knows Um sho is glad to see you lookin' so well. How come you ain' come home 'fo' dis?" When Miss Betty's feet touched the ground, Aunt Betsey's arms went around her, and Miss Betty's arms went around Aunt Betsey.

"Whar dat baby?" she asked almost breathlessly.

"Um's got it," said a quiet, possessive voice from the carriage.

The old woman was taken back. That someone else might share the responsibility, might share the baby before she had "han' picked" that someone herself, had never occurred to her.

With a trifle less confidence she said, "Well, gi' it hyere," and she reached into the darkness.

The nurse hesitated; and Miss Betty, with an excess of youthful caution warned, "Careful, Mammy, don't drop it."

"Drap it?" Aunt Betsey's indignant voice fairly sizzled, "drap it? Miss Betty, whut-in-de-name-uv-Gawd make you think Um gwi dra—?" She laughed, suddenly understanding. "Chilluns," she said, "chilluns." She turned to the nurse—no lack of confidence now, "You gimme dat baby, gal," she commanded, "Ah been han'lin' babies sence 'fo' you er Miss Betty aire one wuz bawn, en Ah knows mo' 'bout 'em right now den whut you ever will know. *Gimme!* Now clear de road, folkses," she called out triumphantly, "Um gwine to Ole Mis'." Bearing the treasure on its pillow, Aunt Betsey led the way.

Early in the afternoon of the following Sunday, Tave, the nurse, and Net strolled about the quarters and showed the baby to the admiring negroes. Aunt Betsey called them into her house and immediately wanted to take the little fellow, but Tave hesitated. Miss Betty had told her not to let anybody have it.

"Don'chu be no fool!" the old woman snapped, "she ain' mean me," and then firmly, "Gimme!"

Aunt Betsey took the baby on her lap and immediately found fault with the way its dress was fastened. She accused Tave of being "kyereless en no'count," and over Tave's protesting "Let dat 'lone, Ai' Betsey, hit's jes right," she was opening the dress at the neck when Tave tried to snatch the baby. The old woman shoved her off, and from within her own waist she drew the red, flannel-wrapped charm she always wore. Waving this before Tave's startled eyes she said fiercely, "Gal, ef you do dat ag'in, Um gwi put a mark on you wid dis whut hit'll take Gawd hisse'f to git off." The frightened girl shrank back in terror, and Aunt Betsey's exploring fingers found something hard around the baby's neck. "Whut's dis?"

she asked, her voice stern, "Whut's dis?" Her fingers brought to light a necklace of chinaberries. "Whar you git dat?" Her voice was unchanged, but her piercing old eyes began to soften. The whimpering Tave explained that someone had sent it to Miss Betty, who had given it to her. "En Ah jes been lettin' 'im wear it a li'l w'ile eve'y day unbeknownst t' Miss Betty, 'ca'se Ah knowed dey wuz good fer teethers. Ah didn' mean no harm, Ai' Betsey," she ended dismally.

The old woman said softly, "You is a good gal, Tave. You ain' done no harm; you is done good. Ah made dat necklis m'se'f. You know," she went on apologetically, "Ah thought you wuz one uv dese ack-uppity town niggers whut think dey know mo' en whut anybody ilse does, but you ain'—you's got sense. Now you en Net run 'long en have a good time wid de young folks, en Ah'll take kyere uv dis baby. Ef he cry, Ah'll know whut t' do. Shoo along now, chillun, *shoo!*" and she shooed the laughing girls away like chickens.

After the girls had gone, she held the cooing baby on her lap. "Whutchu say t' me?" she asked it. "Ah ain' hyeah you dat time, Honey. Whut wuz it? Tell Mammy, tell yo' ole black Mammy whutchu say." She played with the child a while, then began to mutter happily to herself: "No wunner dis chile been havin' a easier time wid his teethes—whut wid dat mice on de tree en w'arin' dat necklis whedder er no. Dat Tave girl sho ain' de fool Ah thought she wuz—she *is* got sense—en Um gwi tell Ole Mis' so, jes ez soon ez Ah go t' de house. Now you come on hyere, boy," she said, gathering the baby up in her arms, "Um gwi show you t' sump'm en show sump'm t' you." She took him to the little elm that was the name-tree and let the branches tickle his face until he smiled. Then she laid him on the ground beneath it "to draw strengt' f'um de ye'th." The sun shining on him through the little limbs of the tree brought strength also. "Good, good," she said happily, "Good two ways—strengt' f'um on High en strengt' f'um de groun', en Um gwi do dis eve'y day, too, jes ez long ez he hyere. Le's go back in de house now, Honey," she said tenderly, "yo' mammy's gwine put you t' sleep."

In the house she used a straight-backed chair as a rocker, and the tap of its legs on the floor punctuated her crooning song:

> "Go—t' sleep,—go—t' sleep,
> Go—t' sleep,—li'l ba—by.
> Daddy's—gone—away,
> Mammy—wouldn'—stay,
> Lef'—nobo—dy home—but de—ba-a—by.
> Go—t' sleep,—go—t' sleep
> Go—t' sleep—li'l ba—by,
> When—you—wake
> You—kin—have—some—cake,
> Go—t' sleep—li'l Ba-a—by."

John tightened his fingers around the red "charm" that hung from Aunt Betsey's neck, snuggled closer to her soft bosom, and with a sigh of content, closed his eyes.

THE CHILD

DE SUN DO MOVE

Six-year-old John, recovering from a severe attack of measles, was making a long visit to his Uncle John and Aunt Sallie at their home in the country. The doctor had prescribed a year in the country and play, but before the year was up John lost his father, and now the visit was to lengthen from one year to several.

During the preceding years he had kept in touch with Aunt Betsey, Net, and some of the older negroes. Now after the first few weeks of his visit, he knew all the negro uncles and aunties, children, and dogs on the place. His days were spent in frolics, but the most fun of all was to be allowed to go with Net, now his trusted guide and caretaker, on their numerous excursions to the negro quarters, to hear tales of "slav'y times" and ghosts and witches. John's unfailing politeness and child-ish courtesy to the older people and his pockets full of teacakes and goodies for young and old alike made his visits welcome ones. Since he had for months only negro playmates by day and had listened almost nightly to tales of "de old folks," their dialect had become his own. Generally, "he spoke the language of the tribe."

When the negroes made frequent reference to his nice behavior, Aunt Betsey unfailingly took due and undue credit to herself. She was willing to divide honors with his grandmother but would go no further than that. "Yeah," she would say, "he *is* a *mighty* good chile—me en Ole Mis', us see to dat—en ef Ah do say so m'se'f, Ah nevuh *is* seed a mo' *mannersly* chile in m' life, not even his mammy whut Ah he'p Ole Mis' to raise. Um tellin' her all de time, Um is, dat ef you raise 'em t' be kin', dey'll be kin', en she 'gree wid me, she do, en dat's whut us is doin'."

If any of her listeners doubted or wanted to smile at her claims, they were careful to keep both doubt and smile hidden, because—well, because Aunt Betsey *could* do things.

John came from the direction of Aunt Betsey's house in search of her; he needed her. Finding the kitchen closed and Aunt Betsey gone he sought Net who was sweeping the yard with a long broom made of persimmon brush.

When he had first come to stay in the country he had been thin from his long spell of sickness, but now his face was round and his body plump—almost too plump. Aunt Emily, who gave him lots of warm milk to drink each milking time, called him her "li'l w'ite calf"; Aunt Betsey called him her "li'l pig" and fed him cookies; and Net, whose duty it was to keep him clean, said he was part calf and part pig, "but de bigges' part uv 'im mus' be mud-turkle 'ca'se ef he cain' fin' a mudhole t' play in, he'll sho make one."

He stood looking into Net's laughing face, cheeks rosy, blue eyes clear, a picture of health. He had lost his hat somewhere, and his thick blonde hair falling over his forehead made a ragged line above his eyes—ragged because his puppy in their game of "pull de rag" had chewed it off. "Net," he asked anxiously, "where Ai' Betsey?"

"She at home, Baby. She lef' jes a little w'ile 'fo' you come."

"Naw she ain't, I jus' come from there," he answered.

"Whutchu want wid her?"

"I wants to ast her somethin', Net, an' now she ain't here." His rising tones promised tears.

"Well, well, well, Baby, you knows de way to Ai' Nervy's house," said Net, "en dat's whar she at ef she ain' at home, 'ca'se she said she 'uz gwine dar dis e'nin'. Whutchu wan' t' ax 'er?"

"I wants to ast her somethin'—," but he was gone.

John's mind was troubled. Bird had told him something that couldn't be true. Yet, Bird knew a "mighty heap" of things. So, following a custom that, so far as he was concerned, began with time, he was asking Aunt Betsey—she knew. He could ask Grandma, of course; she knew everything, but sometimes she laughed at signs and such, and that was bad luck. Aunt Betsey said so.

He found Aunt Betsey and Aunt Nervy seated on the little porch, sheltered by a thick mass of gourd vines. Paying no attention to Aunt Nervy's welcoming smile, he tried to plunge into the matter at once. "Ai' Betsey," he said, "the sun does rise every mornin', don't it?"

She looked at him with disapproval. "Whar yo' manners, Baby?" she asked gently, indicating Aunt Nervy with her eyes.

John was embarrassed to have forgotten his "manners," but his discomfort was lost in Aunt Nervy's smile of approval. "Good e'nin', Ai' Nervy," he said with momentary dignity, "is you well?" and then he turned to Aunt Betsey. "Ai' Betsey, the sun does rise eve'y mornin', don't it?"

"Co'se hit do, Honey. You ain' miss seein' it narry mo'nin' yit, is you?" she asked, amusedly.

"An' it don't stan' still an' us move, do it?"

"Baby, whut *is* you talkin' 'bout? Ah's been livin' a mighty long time, Ah is, en ez long ez Ah been livin' Ah ain' got de 'membrance uv seein' hit miss narry time yit, en you ain', needer. Co'se hit rises en sets, too. Whut make you ax me dat?"

"Bird say it don't rise a-tall. He say it stands still an' the worl' jus' turns over an' over an' over an' folks jus' thinks it rises."

"He say dat, does 'e? Whut in de name uv Gawd kin' uv foolishmint is dat, anyhow?" she asked frowningly, no laughter in her voice now.

"I 'o' know'm. An' he say the worl' ain' flat, either. He say it's roun' like a ball an' just turns over an' over an' don't *never* stop."

"Ah knowed it! Ah knowed it! Jes listen t' dat, Sis Nervy. Ah been tellin' dese folkses dat nothin' but sin en sor'r 'ud come f'um lettin' dese hyere young niggers play ball." Her voice was high-pitched in indignation. "Hit's de devul's own game," she went on, "dat's whut hit is, en now look whut hit's done l'arnt 'em—dat de worl' ain' flat—naw, hit's roun' jes lak a baseball. Jesus, Marster, save us! Whut is us comin' to now?" she asked, looking heavenward. "Sis Nervy, Ah wuz jes tellin' Sis Em'ly no longer ago 'n yistiddy dat a heap a dese hyere sinful young niggers had a heap mo' better be prayin' den runnin' roun' playin' ball. Ah sho wuz tellin' 'er dat. En look whut hit done l'arnt 'em now. You see, don'chu? Um p'intedly gwine speak uv dat at prayer-meetin' t'morrow night, Sis Nervy, Um sho is."

This heresy, coupled with Aunt Betsey's vehemence, shocked Aunt Nervy into silence, but John wanted to tell something else.

"Bird say—," he began.

"Nemmine whut *he* say. Um gwi say sump'm t' Ole Mis' en Ah boun'ju she gwi say sump'm 'bout yo' playin' wid dese no'count, half-growed, eddycated, ball-playin', sinful young niggers whut 'ud be a heap mo' better off ef dey wuz out in de fiel' wuckin' f'um sunrise t' sunset 'nstid uv gwine roun' talkin' sich foolishmint ez dat. Why, Honey, dat's p'intedly 'g'inst de Bible, ain't it? Ah ax you, now ain't it? Answer me dat."

"Yessum," John answered very dutifully.

"Co'se hit is. De Bible say de sun rises in de mo'nin' en sets in de e'nin' en dat nigger say hit don' move. Who you gwi b'lieve? Dat nigger er de Bible? Joshu-a p'inted at de sun en made hit stan' still. How he do dat ef hit ain' movin'? O-o-h, Ah ain' eddycated en Ah cain' read ner write, but Ah done listen to Ole Mis' read a heap, en Ah ain' fergit *nothin'*. Dat *fool* nigger! So de worl' ain' flat nowadays, hunh? Hit's roun' lak a ball! Lawd Gawd, whut is dey gwi say nex'? Now Um gwi ax you sump'm ilse. Don' de Bible speak uv de fo' corn-ders uv de ye'th? Hit do, don't it? Um axin' you now. Don't it?"

"Yessum."

"En ain' de Eas' one cornder, en de Wes' anudder en de Norf one, en de Souf de udder'n? Answer me dat."

"Yessum."

"Well, den. You cain' fin' no cornders on a baseball, kin you? You know you cain't. 'Sides dat, ef de worl' is turnin' over, howcome hit is us don' fall off eve'y night? Naw, Baby, hit's 'g'inst de Bible en hit don' stan' t' reason, hit don't. De 'postle Paul tole one man dat whut li'l eddycation he had done sot 'im crazy, en dat's hol'in' good twel yit. Eddycation is all right fer some folks, but w'en hit comes to dese Bible-'sputin', smart young niggers, you kin gi' *dem* all de eddyca-tion *dey* needs wid a plow-line. Some uv my chillun, de las' uns, kin read en write good, but Ah lay you, you don' hyeah dem talkin' no sich foolishmint ez dat, 'ca'se dey know good en well—don' kyere if dey is full growed en mar'ed en got

chillun uv dey own—Ah'd take a well-rope er a stick uv stove
wood en lam some sense into 'em. Ah would dat.

"Now you listen to me, Sis Nervy. Eddycation is all right
fer white folks; you don' hyeah dem talkin' no sich foolishmint lak dat 'bout de worl' bein' roun'—dey knows hit's flat
Ner dey don' say de sun stan' still. Dey's got sense—dey knows
jes lak eve'ybody ilse does, hit moves f'um Eas' to Wes' eve'y
day en don' nevuh miss. But a nigger—he know mo' en whut
de ole folks do jes ez soon ez he kin read en write 'is name.
W'en you eddycate him you jes done made a no'count, uppity,
know-it-all out'n 'im en sp'ilt a good fiel' han' t' boot. En dat's
Gawd's own trufe."

SPIDER-BITTEN

John lay on Grandma's bed with eyes swollen tight shut and
head and face swathed in bandages. The pain was gone from
his face; his eyes had stopped hurting, too, and, with a long-
drawn sigh, he dozed off.

About the middle of that afternoon Glancey, Uncle Alford's
grown young son, had been sent to clean old Charlie's stable,
and John went with him "to help." While he was playing in
the dark corners of an unused stall, a spider bit him on the
cheek. His screams soon roused the place, and from every part
of the quarters came the negro women to stand in little frightened groups outside the yard and offer innumerable suggestions and cures to Aunt Betsey. They advised her to put on
wet snuff or a chew of tobacco; to apply a cow's cud; to blister
with hot salt or with turpentine and a hot smoothing-iron;
to split open the back of a live black chicken and to bind it on
as you would for snake-bite. Soon Aunt Betsey brought herself back to normal with a jerk. "Listen t' me cah'in' on lak a

fool whilest Miss Sallie en Ole Mis' is wuckin'," she mumbled. From then on she was their very efficient right hand. Only once that afternoon did she leave the boy's bedside, and then just long enough to examine the name-tree. She came back happier; the name-tree was sound and healthy. If that child was going to die, the name-tree would know it beforehand and begin to droop; but now every limb and leaf were green.

Net cooked supper so that Aunt Betsey could stay with John, and when it was ready, the old woman insisted that Grandma eat with the rest of the family. "Me en baby'll git along fine, *won't us?*" she asked him suddenly.

He smiled a crooked, swollen smile and answered slowly, "Yessum."

Grandma put out the light; she was afraid it would hurt his swollen eyes, already weak from measles. When the room was dark and Grandma gone Aunt Betsey asked, "Well, whut is us gwi talk about?"

"I don' know'm," he answered and then whimpered, "I can't see, Ai' Betsey."

"You don' ha' t' see, Baby. Whutchu wan' t' see fer w'en you kin feel me en Ah kin feel you? 'Sides dat, you kin hyeah me en Ah kin hyeah you en dat's enough fer anybody, ain't it? Now," she went on, "whilest Ole Mis' en dem's gone to dey supper, hit's a good time t' tell you dat tale us 'uz talkin' 'bout. Does you 'member?"

"Yessum, Ai' Betsey," John answered, inching closer to the edge of the bed and reaching for her hand, "Yessum, I 'members it. It was 'bout Brer Rabbit."

"Hit wuz?" she questioned, "Le' me see—hit wuz 'bout Brer Rabbit, fer a fac', but whut 'bout 'im? Ah fergits."

"'Bout Brer Rabbit's pop-eyes, Ai' Betsey. Don'chu 'member?" John asked eagerly.

"You right, you right, you sho is right. Well, dat come 'bout in dis way. Brer Rabbit allus wuz smart, he sho wuz, en

eve'ybody gi'n it out, dey did, dat he wuz de smartes' somebody whut live in de woods. But Brer Rabbit wa'n't satterfied;
he kep' wantin' mo' sense. Ah don' know howcome he wuz
dattaway, but he wuz, en right now, dar's a heap a folkses
jes lak 'im—got mo' uv eve'thing 'n whut anybody ilse is got
en ain' satterfied. Well, he worrit 'bout hit, he did, twel fus' en
las', he went t' de kang uv de animuls (some folks say hit 'uz
a witch, en some say hit 'uz Gawd—Ah don' know 'bout dat),
en he ax 'im, he did, t' git him some mo' sense. De kang said
he'd do it, but fus' Brer Rabbit had t' fetch 'im a mess uv
green peas f'um out'n Mist' Man's gyarden. Brer Rabbit say
'Aw right,' en off he went jes lak sump'm wuz atter 'im. He
knowed, he did, dat Mist' Man had a trap sot at de onliest
hole whut 'uz in de gyarden fence; so he jes tuck his walkin'-
stick en prize off anudder palin' somewhar ilse, en in mos' no
time he wuz back at de kang's house wid a big mess uv peas.

"Den de kang say, 'You *is* a smart man, Brer Rabbit, you
sho is, en now w'en Ah come t' think uv it, dar's anudder
thing Ah wants you t' do fer me right off. Ah wants you t' git
me a tail-fedder out'n Brer Buzzu'd's tail; en w'en you come
back wid dat, Um gwi be ready fer you.'

"Brer Rabbit trot off, he did, a li'l bit slower 'n whut he
went de fus' time, 'ca'se he didn' know how he 'uz gwi git
to Brer Buzzu'd t' git dat fedder. Atter wi'le he sot down on
a log 'side uv de road en lit 'is pipe en thunk fer a spell; den
he jump up en run hunt fer Brer Fox. Him en Brer Fox 'uz
good frien's in dem days, en dey run roun' t'gedder a lot.
W'en he tole Brer Fox whut he wanted t' do en ax 'im to
he'p 'im, Brer Fox l-a-f-f, he did, en say he do it. Den him en
Brer Rabbit went out in de fiel', en Brer Fox lay down on de
groun' close t' de brierpatch en stretch out jes lak he daid en
didn' move.

"En w'en he done dat, Brer Rabbit th'owed 'is hat on de
groun' en 'gun to holler en cah'y on en say, 'Brer Fox daid!

U-r-r my Lawd, Brer Fox daid! U-r-r my Lawd, Brer Fox daid!'

"'Twa'n't long den 'fo' all de folkses come roun' en want t' cah'y Brer Fox home. But Brer Rabbit, he wouldn't hyeah to dat. He say dey ha' t' wait fer Brer Buzzu'd t' come en do it, 'ca'se he de un'ertaker. Brer Rabbit wuz still takin' on a mighty lot, he wuz, w'en up come Brer Buzzu'd. Brer Buzzu'd look Brer Fox over, he did, en he say he gwi start beh'yin' 'im right off, en w'ile he 'uz lookin' fer a place to ketch holt uv 'im, Brer Rabbit *snuck* up *b-e-h-i-m-e* 'im en snatch out a han'ful uv dem tail-fedders en lit into de brierpatch! Brer Buzzu'd 'uz mighty mad, uv co'se, en he tuck out atter Brer Rabbit, he did, en try t' ketch im, but Brer Rabbit wuz too quick fer'm. Whilest Brer Buzzu'd wuz runnin' at Brer Rabbit, Brer Fox got up en snuck off, en w'en Brer Buzzu'd come back dar, Brer Fox 'uz gone, too."

John chuckled. "Whut Brer Rabbit do den, Ai' Betsey?"

"Brer Rabbit waited 'ntwel Brer Buzzu'd lef', en den he tuck de fedders t' de kang en he say to 'im, he did, 'Now gimme some mo' sense.' Den de kang sez to 'im, he sez, 'Brer Rabbit, you sho is got a heap a sense, you is; you is got mo' sense right now den anybody whut Ah ever is see, en Ah wushes, Ah does, dat Ah could gi' you some mo' sense but Ah cain' do it,' he sez, *'onlest* you do jes one mo' thing fer me.' When Brer Rabbit ax 'im whut dat wuz, he say he ha' t' have de pizen teethes f'um Brer Rattlesnake whut live in de aige uv de swamp.

"W'en Brer Rabbit lef' de kang dis time he wa'n't runnin' ner needer trottin'—he wuz walkin' slow; 'ca'se dis wuz one time he knowed he had a job on his han's. He walk along slow, he did, en he thought en he thought en he thought, en den he went en tole Brer Fox whut he ha' t' do en ax 'im to he'p 'im ag'in. But Brer Fox say dat dis time he couldn' do it, 'ca'se Brer Rattlesnake wuz a mighty dange'us pusson en quick tempered wid it; en 'sides all dat, he say he ain' been a member uv de chu'ch long enough hisse'f, he hadn', to feel safe ef he tuck sich a ris' ez dat. 'You know how dat is, Brer Rabbit,' he sez. Brer Rabbit did know, but he wouldn' let on, en he kep' atter 'im to he'p him. But Brer Fox jes wouldn' do it dis time; so he walk off en he thought en he thought en he thought. Den he went home en ax Sis Rabbit whut t' do, en she say she didn' know needer. Atter w'ile he went out in de skirt uv woods back uv 'is house en sot down on a stump en smoke a w'ile en thought a w'ile en den he thought some mo'. En den, de fus' thing you know, he laugh out *loud* en slap 'is thigh wid 'is han's, he did, en went en look fer a swee'gum tree.

"He roll him up a ball uv swee'gum ez big ez yo' fis' is, Baby, en den he went to see Sis Pa't'idge en ax her t' gi' 'im some uv her ole fedders, 'ca'se he wan' t' make sump'm p'utty. She gi'n 'em to 'im, she did, en he stuck 'em all over dat ball uv swee'gum en made a li'l pa't'idge. Den he tied a long straing to it en put it in de path whut went by Ole Brer Rattlesnake's house, en den he shake up de leaves so de ole snake 'ud hyeah 'im, en started draggin' dat li'l pa't'idge down de path.

"Brer Rattlesnake hyearn, he did, en he come out to see what 'twuz. W'en he seed dat li'l pa't'idge, he tuck out atter 'im to ketch 'im 'ca'se he love to eat pa't'idges, he did, spesh'ly lit'l uns. Brer Rabbit pull de straing fas', en Brer Snake got faster, en, fus' en las', he cotch up wid it en op'm his big ole mouf en gi'n a snap en driv dem ole long teethes way down in dat swee'gum, en dar dey stuck! He try to op'm his mouf en couldn' do it! Den he twis' en he turn en he roll en he tie hisse'f in bowknots en he tie hisse'f in hard knots en he quile en he unquile, but hit didn' do no good. He thrash aroun' in de bushes en make a heap a racket, he do, en Brer Rabbit, he come up den lak he jes hyeahd him, en he say, 'In de name uv

Gawd, Brer Rattlesnake, whut *is* de matter *wid you?*' Brer Rattlesnake talk to 'im out'n one cornder uv his mouf, he did, en he say he done got stuck on some swee'gum en he ax 'im to he'p 'im git loose. 'Who you reggin done dat?' Brer Rabbit ax 'im en de ole snake say he didn' know en didn' kyere right den; dat whut he wanted wust uv all wuz to git loose, en den he ax 'im to he'p 'im ag'in. Brer Rabbit look at his mouf good en he say, 'Brer Rattlesnake, de onliest way you ever *is* t' git loose is fer me to break dem teethes.' Dat ole snake done plum gi'n out by now en he say 'Break 'em!' Brer Rabbit tuck his pockitknife en break 'em off, en 'fo' dat ole snake could move atter dat, he grab dat ball uv swee'gum wid dem teethes in it en lope off to de kang. W'en de kang seen him wid dem teethes, he say, 'Brer Rabbit,' he sez, 'dar ain' no nuse uv you axin' fer no mo' sense; Ah jes ain' gwine gi' you no mo, 'ca'se you is got too much already.' W'en he say dat, Brer Rabbit, he try to ack uppity, he did, en 'gun to sass him, en de kang got mad, he did, en grab 'im roun' de nake en choke 'im twel his eyes pop out jes lak you see 'em now, en dey is been dattaway ever sence."

"Whut come uv 'at ole mean rattlesnake, Ai' Betsey?" asked John.

"Lawd, Honey, you go t' sleep. Ah cain' 'member no mo' right now, en 'sides dat, Ah done talk plum out."

"Tell me some more, Ai' Betsey, please ma'm," he begged sleepily.

"Well," she said, "ef Ah does, Ah got t' 'member it fus', en whilest Um's 'memberin' it Um gwi sing you a chune." Then taking the little fellow's hand in both of hers she began to croon a wordless melody; soft and low it was, and beautiful, for Aunt Betsey's crooning sounded like a muffled violin.

When Ole Mis' and Miss Sallie came in from supper John was asleep.

While Aunt Betsey was eating supper, an owl—a screech owl—moaned in the oak that was near the kitchen. "G-g-awd!" she gasped. Before she could recover her startled voice, fresh terror was added when another owl, unmistakably on the roof of the kitchen, moaned in answer. "Chris' Jesus, listen t' dat!" She rushed to the fireplace and with a shovel sent clouds of sparks flying upward. Another moan from the roof and— "Th'ow some salt in de fiah, Net! *Move!* Don'chu hyeah me?" she shrieked. "Do sump'm," she went on, "do sump'm, gal. Squeeze yo' wris' en choke 'em t' death!" Another moan from above. "J-e-s-u-s, listen! Brer Alfo'd, do sump'm! Don' stan' dar wid yo' mouf wide op'm, *do* sump'm!"

Miss Sallie hurried into the kitchen followed by Mars John. "Mammy," she asked in a low, tense voice, "*What* is the matter with you? Hush! Hush! You'll scare that boy to death."

But Aunt Betsey was past "hushing." "O-o-o-h, Miss Sallie," she wailed, "O-o-o-h, Mars John—"; then, as the owl's cry quivered out on the night again, "Jes listen t' dat! Git de g-u-n, Mars J-o-h-n, p-l-e-a-s-e *gitdegun!* Dat means death, ef us don' run it away er killit, en dat baby's already sick en swole up. *Please,* Mars John, *please!*"

Miss Sallie said to get the gun—anything was better than this, and besides, Mammy would be sick herself if this kept up. While Mars John was gone for it, Aunt Betsey spied Uncle Alford, still doing nothing. "Brer Alfo'd," she hissed at him, "Brer Alfo'd, Ah tole you t' do sump'm, en you jes stan' still en ain' move!" Then through clenched teeth came—"S-c-r-r-r!" It sounded like a knife being drawn across the bricks of the fireplace to sharpen it—"S-c-r-r-r! G—a—w—d—lest you, you no'count, wuthless—" Before he could budge, she snatched a stick of stovewood from the box and started for him, "*Move,* nigger!" At the door he ran into Mars John. When he paused— just paused—to apologize, with one eye on the still advancing Mammy Betsey, Mars John handed him the gun. A minute later the persistent owl broke off short its last quiver for the night; it was startled into silence by the flash and roar of Mars John's "12-gauge" loaded with noisy black powder.

Things soon quieted down in the kitchen, but it was an hour before Aunt Betsey would go home, and, then, only after she had had a final look at her "baby chile."

GITTIN' WELL

The morning after John was bitten by the spider, Aunt Betsey was in the kitchen at the regular hour, but the sounds that usually accompanied the preparation of breakfast, the clanging of pans and a burst of song, were conspicuously absent; for Aunt Betsey had enjoined strict silence upon all the servants so that John could sleep.

As soon as breakfast was well under way, she tapped lightly on Ole Mis's door. When it opened she asked, "How's Baby? Good mo'nin', Ole Mis'." A low-voiced consultation followed. "Is he been wake?"

"Yes, a little while ago. He fretted to get up but went back to sleep."

"Dat's good, Ole Mis'. Le' 'm sleep. Is de swellin' gone down?"

It had, some, but not much.

"Gawd f'um Heb'm!" exclaimed the old woman. "En Ah boun'ju he got fever yit, ain't he?"

John still had fever, and Ole Mis' was worried because she said that if he wasn't allowed to get up he would fret and make his fever rise, and if he did get up too soon his fever would rise anyway. "So what am I to do, Betsey?" she asked the old woman.

"Lawd, Ole Mis'," Aunt Betsey answered, "don'chu wu'y

'bout dat none. Ah'll keep dat boy in bed dis day widout no trouble a-tall. You'll see. Call me w'en he wake up, Ole Mis', please ma'm, but ef you kin, you keep 'm sleep twel atter eve'body th'ough wid dey breakfus'. Us gwi feed 'im dis mo'nin', ain't us?"

"Why yes, Betsey," Grandma answered almost cautiously, "I thought a little milk-toast would—"

"Done got de toas' made en de milk is gittin' hot right now," Aunt Betsey broke in triumphantly and then turned toward the kitchen. "Call me w'en he ready, Ole Mis', please ma'm," she begged as she started down the stairway.

Breakfast was over in the dining room and the servants had nearly finished theirs in the kitchen when Uncle Alford stepped in the door, his face wreathed in a smile of anticipation. "Good mo'nin', eve'ybody," he greeted them. "Good mo'nin', Sis Betsey. Sis Betsey, Mars John said—"

"Y-e-h, Ah know whut he said, er ilse you wouldn' be hyere," interrupted Aunt Betsey. "Come en git it, nigger," she added viciously, "come en git it, but you 'member dis: Ah ain' feedin' you alonest 'ca'se Mars John sesso. Naw, s-u-h, dat Ah ain't. Um's jes feedin' you to gi' you strengt' to stan' whut's comin' to you w'en Ah does git holt uv you, you slow-movin', good-fer-nothin', mo'-den-half fiel' nigger."

"Aw, Sis Betsey, Ah—"

"Don' chu 'Aw' me none!" snapped the old woman, "Don'-chu do it. Brer Alfo'd," she continued, fixing him with an eye that all the servants dreaded, "fer t' a-been roun' good-sensed folks ez much ez you is, you is de no-sensedes' nigger man Ah ever is seed in all my life. Las' night you'd a stood dar wid yo' mouf op'm en let dat owul shiver his death call twel Jedg-mint Day en you wouldn'a done nothin'—"

"Ah did, Ah did, Sis Betsey!" Uncle Alford protested vigor-ously, "Ah did! You know Ah—"

With one commanding gesture Aunt Betsey waved him into

silence. "Y-e-a-h, Ah knows whutchu done," she said, still looking at him with intense accusation, "but Ah notice, Ah does,
dat you didn' do nothin' twel Ah got atter you wid dat stick
uv stove wood. *Shet up!*" she hissed as the old man tried to
speak. "Slow you is," the relentless voice went on, "Oh m-y
G-a-w-d! Yes, you is slow. You is slow twel yo' belly git empty
en somebody say 'Eat.' Den you is fas' enough, Gawd knows!"

She motioned to a chair at the table and a few minutes later
put a plate of food before him. "Hyere, nigger, shevel dis in
yo' maw en git out!"

Uncle Alford ate in silence and soon slipped away.

It was not long before Ole Mis' called for John's breakfast,
and leaving Net to finish the dishes, Aunt Betsey carried the
bowl of milk-toast to the sick room.

"Now you go res' a w'ile, Ole Mis'," Aunt Betsey said as she
met John's grandmother in the hall, "Ah'll take kyere uv 'im."

"Baby," she called brightly from the doorway, "look whut
yo' ole Ai' Betsey done fotch you. Now you git yo' mouf set
en le's us eat."

"I wan' t' git up, Ai' Betsey," John whimpered.

"Co'se you does, Honey, uv co'se you does," agreed Aunt
Betsey. "Dat's a sign you is gittin' well, too. But you knows
yo'se'f dat you cain' git up, sick en swole up lak you is. Not on
no empty stummick, you cain't. You know dat. So de fus' thing
is—eat. Den us gwi talk 'bout de res' uv it. Us got a heap uv
talkin' to do, too. Now you come on hyere en eat dis."

After a few mouthfuls John said he didn't want any more.

"Howcome dat now, huh?"

"I don' wan' no more, Ai' Betsey. I wan' to—"

"Baby, yo' Polly cow sho ain' gwi lak dat now," said the old
woman sorrowfully, "she sho ain't. She sont you dat milk
spesh'ly, she did. Dat li'l ole steer calf uv her'n wanted de
strippin's hisse'f, but she kicked 'im 'way en made Sis Em'ly

git 'em fer you. Now ef you don' eat dat milk atter she done sont it to you, she sho is gwi feel bad 'bout it. She sho is dat."

"Whut my calf eat?" asked John, who laid claim to everything that was little on the place.

"Oh, he didn' kyere a-tall soon's he knowed you'z gwi git it. Sis Em'ly gi'n him a heap uv de fus' milk, en he say he could drink mo'n you could, anyhow."

"Can't," said John. "Ai' Em'ly say he can't," and with a gesture of determination he reached for the spoon.

When all the milk and toast had disappeared, John lay back on the soft pillows with a crooked smile and said, "Now le's talk, Ai' Betsey," as he held out his hand to her.

"Talk?" Exclaimed the old woman happily. "Yes, chile, us sho is gwi talk dis day. Us got so much talkin' t' do dat Ah don' know whar t' start, does you?"

"No'm," answered the boy.

"Ah don' know needer, Ah sho don't," said Aunt Betsey. "Ah tell you whut us do," she continued quickly, "Um's got t' go t' de gyarden en git a li'l mess uv peas en greens fer dinner. 'Tain't gwi take me long. En whilest Um is gone, you think 'bout it en Um's gwi think 'bout it. En w'en Ah gits back bofe uv us gwi be ready fer it."

John agreed, but when Aunt Betsey started to leave, he let out a wail, "I wants to git u-u-p!"

Aunt Betsey looked at him speculatively for a moment and then, "Ah knows whut de matter wid you is," she said, "Ah sho does. Ah knows jes zac'ly whut de matter is. You jes so much lak dat ole Brer Rabbit Ah tole you 'bout las' night dat you mus' be kin to 'im. Dat's whut de matter is. You ain' satterfied. Brer Rabbit had mo' uv eve'ything den all de res' uv de folkses but he wa'n' satterfied needer. En whut he git f'um it? *Pop-eyes!*" she snapped in answer to her own question. "En hyere you is," she went on, "wid me en Ole Mis' en Net en all de res' uv de niggers en folkses to be wid you en he'p you, but, jes lak Brer Rabbit, you ain' satterfied needer. Naw, you wan' t' git up en go out en play, wid yo' face all swole up, en me en Ole Mis' en eve'ybody knows ef you do do dat, hit'll grow dattaway. Yes hit will. You wait twel Ah git Ole Mis's han' glass. Ah wants to show you whut you's gwi look lak ef you don' stay in dis bed en 'have yo'se'f."

Aunt Betsey got the mirror from Ole Mis's bureau and held it in front of John's face. "Look at dat," she commanded, "jes look at dat. You knows yo'se'f, you does, dat you don' wan' t' look lak dat all de time. You know dat. Now does you? *Does* you? Answer me dat."

The little fellow was frightened. "No'm," he murmured.

"Ah knowed it. Now you stay hyere en keep quiet whilest Um's gittin' dem peas en greens, en Um's gwi be back in mos' no time. Net gwi cook dat dinner t'day."

With a great show of speed Aunt Betsey hurried away, and she was back in "mos' no time."

With the vegetables gathered and Net installed in the kitchen, Aunt Betsey was soon back in the sick room. "Well, hyere Um is, jes lak Ah tole you," she said, smiling brightly. "En Ah boun'ju you ain' thought uv nothin' fer us to talk about, is you?" she continued.

"No'm," answered the boy.

"Ah knowed it, Ah sho did. Well Um is done thought uv sump'm. Thinkin' is a cu'us sorta thing, Baby" she went on thoughtfully. "Ef you thinks uv one thing hit fetches up an-udder. You thinks uv dat a w'ile, en dat brings sump'm ilse to yo' min' en you thinks uv dat a w'ile, en dat brings sump'm ilse. F'um dat you jumps to sump'm ilse, twel, fus' en las', you come right back to whar you started f'um, jes lak somebody whut's los' in de woods. En dat's jes whut Ah done done. Ah started out thinkin' 'bout Brer Rabbit en all de res' uv 'em, en Ah jes nach'ly come back to him, en hyere us is."

John gave a delighted giggle, and as Aunt Betsey drew her chair close to the bed, he reached for her hand.

"Now," continued the old woman, "dishyere tale is 'bout howcome hit is Brer Rabbit don' ha' t' wuck no mo'. Dat come 'bout dissaway:

"In dem days, mos' lak whut dey does now, folkses all live in settlemints en sich. En dey wuz p'utty good neighbors to one 'nudder, dey wuz, too, en b'lieved in havin' a good time.

"Things 'uz gwine 'long mighty well, dey wuz, twel a big boss li-yon—'de boss uv de woods,' he call hisse'f—move into de settlemint whar Brer Rabbit en Brer Fox en Brer Coon en all de folkses live at. En he didn' do nothin', he didn', but jes lay roun' en 'stroy pigs en goats en things, twel atter w'ile hit look lak he 'uz gwi plum ruin de whole neighborhood en eve'ything in it.

"De folks all got t'gedder, dey did, en hilt a meetin'. En atter a heap uv argymints, fus' dis' way en den dat, dey 'cided dey'd jes ha' t' tell Brer Li-yon dat dey jes couldn' stan' hit no longer, 'ca'se ef he kep' up doin' lak he had been doin', dat fus' en las', dar wouldn' be nobody lef' but jes Brer Li-yon. Dey said dey'd 'gree t' feed 'im, dey would, 'ca'se hit wa'n't right t' starve nobody t' death, but ef dey did feed 'im, he sho ha' t' stay in his house en 'have hisse'f. En ef de didn' wan' t' do dat, dey 'uz gwi be fo'ced to have de law on 'im en maybe put 'im in de callyboose, too.

"Den Brer Fox, he jump up en say, 'Well, gentermens, us is got dis part uv it all settled now. De nex' thing is: Who's gwine cah'y de news to Brer Li-yon?'

"Dat started anudder argymint, 'ca'se dey knowed Brer Li-yon wuz a bad man to fool wid, en dey all wuz skeered.

"Brer B'ar said he wouldn' min' gwine down to Brer Li-yon's house tellin' 'im whut de folkses say, but he say he 'uz already behime wid 'is corn plantin' in 'is new groun', en he jes didn' had de time.

"Brer Fox say he ha' t' go en dig a well 'fo' his stock all pehish fer water, en he couldn' go.

"Dey all gi'n fus' one kin' uv scuse en den anudder. Brer Goose say he jes ha' t' git in 'is fiel' en cut grass; en Brer Gobbler say Sis Turkey wuz down sick wid a mis'ry in 'er back en he had t' git home right away en ten' t' de chillun. Brer Pig said he ha' t' go en root up 'is gyarden 'fo' hit come a rain. Hit look lak all uv 'em had some 'portant business t' ten' to en couldn' none uv 'em cah'y de news to Brer Li-yon.

"Den Brer Rabbit jump up, he did, en pop 'is heels t'gedder, en he say, 'By Gollies, folkses, ef y'all is skeered uv 'im, Ah ain't.'

"Now, Baby," said the old woman, "Brer Rabbit wuz a mighty good man, he wuz, en a mighty smart un, too; but he sho would cuss w'en de 'casion come up. He sho would do dat."

"But, Ai' Betsey," said the puzzled boy, "I didn't know good folks cussed. Uncle John don't do it; an' you don't do it; an' Unc' Alfo'd don't do it."

"Well, you see, Baby, w'en Ah says Brer Rabbit 'uz a good man, Ah means he wuz a good neighbor en kin'-hearted. You never could rightly call Brer Rabbit a good Chris'chun man, you couldn', en 'sides dat, in dem days things wuz some diff'-unt f'um whut dey is now. You see?"

John nodded his head in complete understanding.

"Well," Aunt Betsey went on, "Brer Rabbit he say, 'Folkses,' sezzee, jes shakin' 'is haid f'um side t' side lak he 'uz mad, 'a man's jes a man, en he ain' no mo'n nobody ilse. Um's a man, Um is, jes lak whut Brer Li-yon is. Ah don' kyere ef y'all is skeered uv 'im, Ah ain't. Ah'll take de news to 'im m'se'f.'

"Den de folkses all say, 'Aw shucks, Brer Rabbit, you know you's got more sense 'n t' do dat. Brer Li-yon is two three times bigger'n whutchu is, en he'll eat chu up en won' know he done had a mou'ful. Ain' chu skeered?'

" 'Skeered? Who? *Me?* Why, Gawd bless yo' souls, folkses,

Ah thought y'all already knowed Ah ain' skeered uv nothin' ner nobody. En jes to prove hit to you, Um's gwine down dar en tell dat ole mangy-hided Brer Li-yon jes zac'ly whut us gwine do fer 'im, en jes zac'ly whut us ain't. En ef he don' lak it, he kin jes lump it. You wait hyere fer me, folkses,' sezzee, 'en Ah'll show you.'

"Wid dat, Brer Rabbit tucked 'is britches-laigs down in dem red-top boots uv his'n, pulled his white duck-cloth cap to one side uv 'is haid, en den wid a big see-gyar sho't stickin' out'n 'is mouf he sa'ntered off down de road twoge Brer Li-yon's house, jes lak he 'uz gwine to a picnic.

"Brer Rabbit walk mighty biggity, he did, ez long ez de folkses could see 'im, but w'en he got roun' a ben' in de road, he rub dat see-gyar sho't out 'g'inst a stump en put 'tin 'is pockit, en he straighten' de cap on 'is haid en f'um den on, he walk mighty diff'unt, 'ca'se he wuz skeered en 'is knees 'uz shakin'.

"W'en he got t' de li-yon's house he crope up to de do', he did, en he knock on it easy-lak, 'tap—tap—tap,' en he say 'Mist' Li-yon, Uh-r-r Mist' Li-yon.' En his voice 'uz so weak en trem'ly he couldn' hardly hyeah it hisse'f.

"But de li-yon hyeahd, he did, en he come th'owed de do' op'm en he hollered out *big*, 'WHO IS YOU EN WHUT-CHU WANT?'

"Brer Rabbit 'uz jes shakin'. 'Dis is jes me,' he sez, 'hit's jes Brer Rabbit, Mist' Li-yon. De folkses done had a meetin',' he sez, 'dey done had a meetin' en dey sont me down hyere t' tell you dat—to splain to you dat dey done 'cided—'cided dat, seein' dat you is de big boss uv de whole worl', hit ain' right fer you to ha' t' go out en git yo' vittles. En—en dey done tole me to tell you dat—dat ef you'll stay in yo' house all de time en don' go out fohagin' none, dey'll sen' you sump'm t' eat—dey'll sen' yo' sump'm t' eat down hyere to you. En dat's jes zac'ly whut dey tole me t' tell you, Mist' Li-yon,' he say, squattin' en gittin' ready t' run.

" 'WELL, AH GOT TO HAVE FRESH MEAT THREE TIMES A DAY,' de li-yon hollered at 'im, 'EF DEY'LL DO DAT, AH'LL STAY IN DE HOUSE. BUT EF DEY DON'T, UM GWI 'STROY EVE'YBODY.'

"Brer Rabbit, he say, 'Yassuh, y-a-s-s-u-h, Mist' Li-yon, y-a-s-s-u-h! Dey do dat, sho! Dey gwi feed you good, too, 'ca'se Um's gwi see t' dat m'se'f,' he say.

"Wid dat, Brer Rabbit tuck off down de road, he did, lick-ety-split. Soon ez he wuz out uv sight uv Brer Li-yon he stop en knock de dus' off'n 'is boots, pull de cap down on de side uv 'is haid ag'in, en wid dat ole see-gyar sho't stickin' out one cornder 'is mouf, he strutted back to whar de folkses 'uz waitin' fer 'im at.

"W'en dey seed Brer Rabbit comin', dey all run to meet 'im. 'Is you see 'im?' dey ax 'im. 'Is you seed Mist' Li-yon? Whut he say?'

"Den Brer Rabbit say, right biggity-lak, 'Is Ah seed 'im? Well, Ah went down dar to see 'im, didn't Ah? Howcome you thinks Ah ain' seed 'im, den? Co'se Ah's seed 'im.'

"Den de folkses say, 'L-a-w-d-e-e, Brer Rabbit! You d-i-d? Whutchu tell 'im? Wa'n'chu skeered?'

"W'en dey ax 'im dat, Brer Rabbit snatch 'is cap off'n de side uv 'is haid en th'owed hit down on de groun' en stomp it. 'Skeered,' sezzee, 'whut in de name uv Gawd kin' uv fool-ishmint is you talkin' now? Why, folkses,' sezzee, doublin' up 'is fis' en shakin' it in all dey faces, 'Um's a man, Um is. A m-a-n, a m—a—n, Ah tells you. En being's Um is a man, Ah ain' skeered uv nothin' ner nobody, en dat means Brer Li-yon en all de res'.'

"Den de folkses jes beg Brer Rabbit t' tell 'em all 'bout it.

" 'Well,' sez Brer Rabbit, 'W'en Ah went down to ole Brer Li-yon's house, Ah knock on de do', Ah did, en w'en he op'm it, Ah went in en sot down by de fiah. En Ah tole 'im dat us had done had a meetin' en 'cided dat he wuz raisin' too much 'sturbunce in de neighborhood. En Ah tole 'im us done 'cided he'd ha' t' stay in his house en 'have hisse'f er ilse us 'uz gwi beat 'is Gawd-lested liver out, en de Lawd hisse'f only knowed whut ilse. Den Ah tole 'im us 'ud feed 'im. Ah tole 'im us didn't wan' t' see nobody suffer en starve, so us 'ud feed 'im, us would, but he'd ha' t' take jes whut us wan' t' gi' 'im en be satterfied wid it, er ilse he could jes lump it.'

"Den de folkses all say, 'Lawd, Brer Rabbit, you s-h-o i-s b-r-a-v-e!'

" 'Um's jes a man, folkses,' sez Brer Rabbit, en he pick up his cap en knock de dirt off'n it en sot it back on de side uv 'is haid. 'Jes a man, folkses, dat's all. Ole Brer Li-yon, he pitch en he cuss en he ro'd, but dat didn' skeer me none; en w'en he seed Ah meant business he say he'd do jes whut de folkses tell 'im. En dat's jes how 'twuz.'

"Den de folkses tried to 'cide who gwi be de fus' un t' go en feed Mist' Li-yon. Eve'body said to eve'body ilse, 'You go fus', you go fus', you go fus',' en dar dey stuck.

"Dey arg'ed en qua'el 'mongst d'se'fs twel Brer Rabbit tole 'em, 'Le's draw straws, en de one whut gits de sho't un feeds de li-yon.'

"Dey 'greed t' dat, dey did. Brer Rabbit hilt de straws, en Brer Goose, he drawed de sho't un.

"W'en Brer Goose seed he had de sho't straw, he 'gun to shiver en shake 'is whings en he say, 'N-a-a nah! N-a-a nah!'

" 'Y-e-h yeh!' sez Brer Rabbit, sezzee, 'Y-e-h yeh! Git on down dar en feed Brer Li-yon lak you done 'greed t' do.'

"So Brer Goose went on down dar en Brer Li-yon et 'im up.

"De nex' feedin' time, Brer Pig drawed de sho't straw. W'en he seed he 'uz de nex', he started crynin' en holl'in', 'W-a-i-t! W-a-i-t! W-a-i-t! W-a-i-t!'

" 'W-a-i-t! de devul!' sez Brer Rabbit, sezzee, 'You git on down yon'er en feed Brer Li-yon lak you done 'greed to, ilse us'll beat you half t' death en drag you dar.'

"So Brer Pig went on down dar en Brer Li-yon et *him* up.

"Now Brer Fox en Brer Allygater soon seed dat ez long ez Brer Rabbit hilt de straws he 'uz gwi sen' eve'ybody ilse, cep'm hisse'f, down de road t' feed dat li-yon. So at de nex' feedin' time dey fix it so dat Brer Fox hilt de straws. En sho 'nough, dis time Brer Rabbit, he drawed de sho't un!

"W'en he see he done got de sho't straw, he say t' hisse'f, he did, 'Dar Gawd! Ef Ah ain' sho done got my business in a twis' now.' Den he say out loud, 'Folkses,' sezzee, 'hit sho do look lak my time done come. Us is done had a heap uv fun en frolics t'gedder, us is,' sezzee, 'but dat's behime us now. En now Um's got t' go en feed dat ole li-yon's belly. Ah's been a good frien' t' y'all, folkses,' he sez, 'en a good neighbor, too. Ah vis'ted de sick en fed de hongry en he'p to bury de daid. But now hit looks lak my time's done come, en Ah wants you all to pray fer me en promus me dat w'en yo' time comes you'll all meet me in de Promus' Lan' whar d'ain' no-body goes but de pyo' in heart. Goodbye, folkses, goodbye, eve'body,' sez Brer Rabbit, en den he started walkin' off down de road, slow en mo'nful.

"Brer Rabbit soun' so pitiful dat all de folkses started crynin', en jes 'fo' he got out uv sight roun' a ben' in de road, Brer Houn' Dawg, whut wuz de gospel cah'ier, started singin',

> 'Am I bawn to die,
> To lay dis body down?'

en eve'body j'ined in.

"Brer Rabbit, he walk along mighty slow, he did, en den he 'cided dat, even ef ole Mist' Li-yon did ha' t' wait fer his dinner, he 'uz gwi look over his big plantation one mo' time anyhow.

"Soon ez he 'cided dat, he tuck off th'ough de woods to 'is house. W'en he got dar, he went all roun' en roun'. He went t' whar he wuz bawn at, en he went t' de barn en de hawg-lot en de gyarden, en he said goodbye to eve'ything. En den he went t' de well fer a las' drink a water. He look over in dat ole deep well uv his'n, he did, en w'en he seed his own face shinin' up at 'im f'um de bottom, hit gi'n 'im a idee. So he slap his laig wid his han's en slam de kiver shet, he did, en put out th'ough de woods fer de ole li-yon's house. W'en he got dar hit 'uz way atter one by de clock.

"He knock on de do', he did, en he say, 'Mist' Li-yon,' he say, en his voice 'uz weak en trem'ly, 'U-r-r-r Mist' Li-yon, hyere yo' dinner.'

"De ole li-yon th'owed op'm de do', he did, en he ro'd out, 'WELL, HIT'S A MIGHTY LI'L DINNER YOU DONE FOTCH ME, EN HYERE HIT IS 'WAY ATTER ONE O'CLOCK.' En den Brer Li-yon pull out his big gol' watch en look at it, en he showed Brer Rabbit his tushes.

"Brer Rabbit look at dem big ole tushes stickin' out'n Ole Brer Li-yon's mouf en 'is knees shuck wuss'n ever. Den he say, 'Yassuh, Mist' Li-yon, yassuh. Ah jes couldn' gitchere no sooner, Ah couldn'. Um is mighty sorry, Mist' Li-yon, ef Ah ain' enough fer yo' dinner; but ef you is r-a-l-e hongry—hongry, Ah knows whar dar is a h-e-a-p uv good fresh—fresh meat Ah done save fer you. En Ah'll show hit to you, too, ef'n you'll come go—go wid me. En dat's de Gawd's trufe, Mist' Li-yon, hit sho is,' sezzee.

"'WHAR IS DAT MEAT AT?' de ole li-yon ax 'im.

"'Hit ain' fur, Mist' Li-yon,' sez Brer Rabbit, sezzee, 'hit ain' but jes a li'l piece—jes a li'l piece over t' my house whar Ah got—got hit put up fer you.'

"'WELL, HIT BETTER BE ENOUGH!' sez de ole li-yon, sezzee, en wid dat, him en Brer Rabbit put out th'ough de woods to Brer Rabbit's house.

"Brer Rabbit op'm de well, he did, en look in it en fell back! 'L-a-w-d G-a-w-d!' sezzee, 'ef he ain' in dar eatin' yo' vittles right now!'

"When Brer Rabbit say dat, de ole li-yon knock 'im 'way f'um de well en look down it hisse'f. He thought he seed anudder li-yon lookin' up at 'im en he hollered, 'WHO IS YOU?'

"De voice come back up out'n de well, 'WHO IS YOU?'

"Ole Brer Li-yon 'gun to git mad an he hollered down de well ag'in, 'WHO IS YOU, AH SAY?'

"En de voice come back up out'n de well, 'WHO IS YOU, AH SAY?'

"Den Brer Rabbit nudge de ole li-yon in de side en he say, 'You hyeahd 'im, didn'chu, Brer Li-yon? Didn'chu hyeahd 'im mockin' you lak dat? Gawd-lest 'is soul!' sez Brer Rabbit, sezzee, doublin' up 'is fis' en dancin' roun' t' de udder side uv de well f'um de ole li-yon. 'Is you gwi take dat? Is you? Is you gwi take dat slack talk f'um 'im, Brer Li-yon? C-o-r-n-f-o-u-n' 'is fresh-meat-stealin' soul,' sezzee, 'ef he'll come up hyere Ah'll whup 'im 'm'se'f!' he say.

"De ole li-yon look over in de well ag'in en he hollered, 'WHO-O-O-O-O-O-O-O-O—!'

"De voice come back up out'n de well, 'WHO-O-O-O-O-O-O-O—!'

"Den de li-yon say, 'STAN' BACK, BRER RABBIT,' sezzee, 'HE'S MY MEAT!' En in he jump.

"Soon ez Brer Rabbit hyeahd 'im hit de water—Kerchug!—he slam de kiver shet en lock it. Den he pulled his cap t' one side uv 'is haid, tuck dat see-gyar sho't out'n 'is pockit en lit it, en den he sa'ntered on down de road to whar de folkses wuz 'batin' 'bout who wuz t' feed de li-yon nex'.

"When dey fus' seed Brer Rabbit comin', dey thought he wuz a ha'nt, en dey started to run. But he stop 'em, he did,

en den dey all ax 'im en say, 'Lawd, Brer Rabbit, ain' Mist'
Li-yon et you up?'

"En Brer Rabbit say, 'Et who up? Me? N-a-w Gawd! Ah
wa'n't aimin' to be et up by dat durned ole li-yon ner nobody
ilse.'

" 'But whut he s-a-y, Brer Rabbit? En whut de do? Ur-r-r
my Lawdy, Mist' Li-yon gwi come up yere terreckly, jes lak
he say, en 'stroy all us!'

"Den Brer Rabbit laugh mighty biggity, he did, en he say,
'D'ain' no nuse in you folkses bein' skeered uv nothin' ez long
ez you got a man wid you,' sezzee, 'en dat's me. Um's a man,
folkses, jes lak Ah said. En w'en Ah sez Um's a man Ah
means Um is a man, en Ah kin prove it. Dat big ole fool li-yon
ain' said nothin', he ain' done nothin' en he ain' gwi 'stroy
nothin', 'ca'se w'en he tried t' git raw wid me, Ah beat de low-
down scoun'l half t' death en th'owed 'im in my well en
drown 'im.'

"De folkses wouldn' b'lieve 'im, dey wouldn', twel Brer
Rabbit tuck 'em all over to 'is house en op'm de well en showed
'em de ole li-yon down in de bottom all drownded.

"Den dey all say, 'Brer Rabbit,' say dey, 'You is too smart a
man to be anything cep'm a kang. En f'um dis time on, you
ain' nevuh gwi ha' t' wuck no crop, 'ca'se us is gwi do it
fer you.'

"En dat's jes zac'ly howcome hit is, dat f'um dat day twel
dis, Brer Rabbit been livin' on udder folkses' goobers en taters
en things."

John's happy chuckle soon turned into a request for more.
With a look of surprise the old woman asked, "Mo' whut?"
"Mo' 'bout Brer Rabbit, Ai' Betsey."
"My Lawd, Boy! Ain'chu hyeahd 'nough 'bout him?"
"No'm."
"Yes, you is. But Ah tell you whut Ah is gwi do. Um's gwi

"Ole Brer Li-yon hollered down de well"

sing you dat song whutchu lak so 'bout Brer Frawg went a-cotin'. Dat's a good un, ain't it"

It was one of John's favorites. "Ye'm," he answered drowsily.

"Aw right, den. Butchu knows Ah cain' sing les'n hit's sorta dark," said Aunt Betsey, "so Um's gwine pull dese curtain-shades down."

Presently she began to sing in a low, crooning, sleepy tone:

> "Frawg went a-co'tin', he did ride, ah-hum.
> Frawg went a-co'tin', he did ride,
> Swode en pistol by his side, ah-hum."

She sang the song through its many verses, but long before she reached the end, John was asleep.

"Ole Mis'," she whispered, as Grandma came tiptoeing into the room, "de fever's leavin' 'im; his han's is startin' to sweat." Then she added softly, "Us knows chilluns, don't us, Ole Mis'?"

'SPE'ENCE

John's first lesson in practical experience to be remembered as such was learned at Aunt Betsey's house one afternoon. He had broken a green gourd she had given him to play with, and the seed, pumpkin-like in appearance, and the white, pulpy meat must have looked inviting. Anyway, some of the substance soon found its way into his mouth and—out!

Those who have tasted a green gourd know that its nasty bitterness is without a rival. Quinine is like sugar and a dose of castor oil a pleasure in comparison.

Aunt Betsey laughed immoderately at the face John made and stopped only when she saw he was on the verge of tears.

"Dar now, Baby, you'd laugh yo'se'f ef you could see de face you makin'. You look jes lak dis." The screwed-up face she turned toward him was funny; and he laughed a little, but not much. "Ah coulda tole you hit wuz bitter," she went on, "but you'da ha' t' ta'se hit anyhow. De burnt chile is skeered uv fiah, en atter one ta'se uv green go'd he skeered uv dat, too. 'Spe'ence is de bes'." John was trying with both hands—and small success—to wipe the bitter taste off his tongue.

"Whut's 'spe'ence, Ai' Betsey?" he mumbled between scrapes.

"'Spe-ence, Honey, is er-r—." She was puzzled for a moment and then snapped—"Don'chu know whut 'spe'ence is?"

"No'm. Uncle John say 'spe'ence is the best teacher, an' I ast 'im if she was a woman er a man an' he said, 'Both son, but mostly women,' en Auntie laughed at 'im. Is she, Ai' Betsey?"

"Mars John tole you right, Baby, dat is, ez fur ez he went. 'Spe'ence is whut you gits w'en you won' l'arn by listenin' to whut de ole folks tells you. You ought t' listen t' dem all de time, Honey. Dey knows. Now, ef Ah had a tole you dat go'd wuz bitter—mighty bitter—en you had a b'lieved me, dat 'ud been l'arnin' by listenin'. Ah knowed you wouldn', dough, en Ah let you put 'tin yo' mouf. Dat's l'arnin' by tas'in', en dat's *jes whut 'spe'ence is*—l'arnin' by tas'in'. Mos' uv de bitterness en sor'r in dis hyere life 'ud pass us by ef us let it. But naw— all us got to have a tas'e. One tas'e is enough fer some folks. Dey l'arns quick. En udders say de nex' go'd gwine be sweet en jes keep a-tas'in' en don' nevuh l'arn. You cain' he'p dem kin'. But mos' fo'ks soon l'arn dat go'ds wa'n't put yere to be et ner yit to be tas'ed. Tchee!" she snickered, "you know dat now, don'chu? You sho is l'arnin' fas', too," and she laughed outright.

"Whut go'ds put here for, Ai' Betsey?"

"Oh, a heap a things, Honey. Sometimes dey's good fer chillun t' tas'e—you know dat a'ready—den dey's good fer soap-dishes, er dippers, er martin nes'es, er baby rattles en a heap a things. But mos'ly, dey's good t' keep snakes 'way f'um de house."

"You said sunflowers was good fer that."

"Dat's so, too, Honey; dey is, dey sho is. Ah didn' tell you wrong den, en Ah ain' nevuh gwi' do dat. Snakes jes nach'ly don' lak sunflowers en won' stay roun' 'em; but w'en he fin' a go'd vine at yo' do', he jes h'ist his tail, he do, en gits 'way f'um dar lickety-split, 'ca'se he know hit ain' no place fer him. En he tell all de udder snakes too—dey kin talk to one anudder, dey kin, jes lak eve'ything ilse does—en ef you hap'ms to see a snake aroun' atter dat, hit'll be jes one d'dat snake hap'ms to miss. En dat's de Gawd's trufe."

"Does snakebites hurt you, Ai' Betsey?"

"*Does* dey *hurts* you? L-a-w-d G-a-w-d, Honey, yes! Dey kills you, dat's all."

"Well, Bird caught me a green one the udder day an' it didn't bit none. He jus' stuck out his tongue."

"Now hyere, Honey," Aunt Betsey said very earnestly, "you jes listen to me. All snakes bites you 'ca'se Gawd made 'em dattaway. Dey bites you w'en you lookin' en dey bites you w'en you ain' lookin', don' kyere whedder dey's green er red er black er whut. You quit foolin' wid dem snakes whut dat fool Bird nigger fetches you. Uv co'se dey'll bite you, Honey. Hit's ag'ins' nachur fer 'em not to. Dey's all got a fockit tongue jes lak de devul's pitchfork is, en dat's a sign Gawd done gi'n you to know dey sho is kin to 'im."

"But, Ai' Betsey, all snakes don't bite you, now does they?"

"*Yes* dey *do,* Honey, *yes dey do—all* uv 'em—rattlesnakes er moccasins er spreadin' adders er j'inted snakes er chicken snakes er *all* uv 'em, dey do, en den dar's bull snakes en hoop snakes. Dey don' bite you—de bull snake jes ties hisse'f roun' you en whups you to death wid 'is tail. En a hoop snake— Lawd, Honey, ef you sees one uv dem comin', you jes leave dar, 'ca'se he rolls lak a hoop, en he's got a stinger in 'is tail, en ef he pop dat in you, dar ain' no he'p fer you—you gone *sho,* 'ca'se hit's sartin death. Cain' nothin' save you."

"D'ju ever see one, Ai' Betsey—a hoop snake, I mean?"

"Is Ah? Is Ah seed a hoop snake? H-m-many's de times! Lawd, Honey, Ah's seed eve'ything! Back in ole Ferginny onest w'en Ah wuz a gal, a hoop snake got atter me one day w'en Ah wuz comin' f'um de fiel' whar Ah been to cah'y some sweeten' water to de choppers whut Ole Mis' done make me made 'em, en hit mos' cotch me, hit did, en Ah ha' t' dodge b'hime a water-oak tree whut wuz mos' big ez my wais'. En dat ole snake lam 'is stinger in dat tree, he did, en stuck dar. En Ah call de folks f'um de corn-fiel' whar dey wuz choppin' en dey come up dar en kill 'im. Dey wuz skeered t' pull dat stinger out'n de tree, dey wuz, en leffit, en de ve'y nex' day dat tree wuz daid! You 'member dis, Honey, en you be aw right. Don' you fool wid no mo' snakes ner nothin' lak dat. But ef you do hap'm to git bit by one, you make 'em ketch a black chicken en split 'is back op'm w'ile he's live en slap hit on whar you's bit, en hit'll draw de pizen out. Atter dat chicken been on dar a li'l w'ile, hit'll turn right green. W'en hit do dat, de pizen's all out. But de bes' thing is *don' git snakebit*—en you won't ef you stay 'way f'um em en let 'em alone. 'Member dat go'd, Honey, en don' you be one uv dese hyere folkses whut jes keep a-tas'in'. L'arn by listenin', 'ca'se one tas'e uv snakebite en you might swell up en bus' en den us ha' t' dig a hole en beh'y you.

"Now come on, Honey, en le's go t' de house—hit's mos' time fer t' start supper."

PALS

PALS

John stood in the back yard looking through the fence at a game of ball between some little negroes whose only clothing was a long shirt that came to their knees—"shu't-tail," they called it. He wasn't permitted to leave the yard without escort, and the negro children weren't allowed in the yard without "britches," so that all he could do now was to watch. "John! O-o-h John!" Miss Sallie's voice was calling but John didn't hear.

When Miss Sallie called a second time, Aunt Betsey answered, "Ah'll git 'im fer you, Miss Sallie."

"I only want to know where he is, Mammy. Where is he and what is he doing?"

Aunt Betsey's tone was resentful. "He's out yon'er in de back yard, Miss Sallie, en he's lookin' th'ough de fence— lookin' th'ough de fence at dem nigger chillun playin' when he ought t' be playin' wid 'em, er ilse, dey playin' wid him."

"Why doesn't he play with them, then?" she asked. "He knows I don't care if he does that."

"Yessum, Ah reggin he knows dat. But you done tole 'im not t' go outside de yard en he ain' gwi do it; en you done tole dem chillun dey cain' come in de yard wid nothin' but dey shu't-tails on, en dey ain' gwi do dat, needer. Dey ain' got no britches dey kin wear eve'y day in de summer time, Miss Sallie, en hit's too hot, anyways; so whut kin dat po' chile do but jes look th'ough de fence?"

Miss Sallie was worried and looked it; her own playtime wasn't so far away that she couldn't understand. "Well, Mammy," she asked, "What can we do about it?"

"Ah don' know'm, Miss Sallie, les'n us—" she pondered a minute and then said quickly, "Ah know! Le's us git 'im a nigger fer his own se'f! Dar's some likely young niggers in dat passel uv chillun dat plays roun' de yard, Miss Sallie, en us kin go right now en pick out one t' play wid dat chile all de time; en 'sides dat," she went on, "us needs anudder young nigger roun' de yard anyhow."

They found the children behind the stable in the far corner of the yard and listened to what they were saying. The ball game was over, and all the boys had gone back to the quarters except one. He was about three years older than John, and his yellow skin held a decided tinge that suggested his Indian ancestry. He was talking, and his eyes looked adoringly through the fence at John and John returned his look in kind.

"Ah sho do wush Ah could come in dar en play wid you, fel-ler," he was saying, "but Mammy jes won' le' me w'ar dem britches no days in de summer time cep'm Sundays. Dat's jes day atter t'morrow, dough, en Sunday mo'nin' *soon*—'fo' you git yo' breakfus'—Um gwi put on dem britches en come over dar en us ain' gwi do nothin' *all day* cep'm jes play, is us?"

John squirmed with delight, "Uh-huh, yeah, en us won' stop hardly fer dinner, will us, Henry?" he asked.

"Us ha' t' stop den, Ah reggin," said Henry. Then he went on wistfully, "You reggin Miss Sallie won' make Ai' Betsey gi' me some dinner?"

"Yeah, an if she don't, I'll gi' you some uv mine, Henry," promised John.

"You haves cake eve'y Sunday, don'chu?" he asked.

"Yeah, an' mos' ev'ry day, too, an' nex' Sunday us goin' have ice-cream, I spec'," said John, ready to promise anything.

"Lawdy, sho' nough?" Henry could say no more.

Aunt Betsey turned to the listening Miss Sallie: "Dat's de one us is lookin' fer, Miss Sallie," she said in an undertone, "dat's Amy's Henry, en he done picked hisse'f. You tell 'im."

When Miss Sallie and Aunt Betsey came around the corner of the stable, Henry was startled and jumped up, poised for instant flight; but when he saw Miss Sallie's eyes he smiled.

"You are Amy's boy, aren't you?" she asked.

"Ye'm." He was changing his balance from one foot to the other, his eyes roving in embarrassment.

"Is she at home?"

"Ye'm."

"What's your name?"

"Henry Po'ter."

"Do you like my little John?" she asked.

His slight movement toward John was instinctively protective. His face was serious for a moment, and then his eyes met Miss Sallie's without a waver. "Ye'm," he answered and Miss Sallie was satisfied.

"Do you want to come and stay at the yard and play with him all the time?"

"Ye'm."

"And do you think you can play with him and not let him get hurt?" she asked him; but, before he could answer, Aunt Betsey added, "En you ain' gwi hu't 'im yo'se'f, is you, nigger?"

"Ye'm," said Henry, looking at Miss Sallie, and then glancing at Aunt Betsey, he answered her, "No'm."

"Do you want him?" Miss Sallie then asked John, who was trembling with excitement. His dancing eyes answered for him and she continued to Henry, "Well, then, go home and put on your breeches, and tell Amy you are going to stay at the yard and that I'll see to your clothes."

Henry looked at John and with a happy, exultant "Hah!" was off like the wind. Halfway home he turned to wave and send back another "Hah," and was off like the wind again.

When he came back a few minutes later, John met him at the gate; and with his arm around Henry's waist and Henry's arm around his shoulder, they danced up the walk to the house, laughing at nothing and happy—they were "Pals."

JOHN DE BAPTIS'

G-w-o-n 'way f'um me, John de Baptis'—John de devul us ought t' be callin' you, you mannish, no-mannered—Go 'w-a-y f'um hyere—! Baby!" Aunt Betsey was in distress and mad too—even the dullest ears could tell that. "B-a-a-by! Ef you don' come on hyere en git dis—. Dar now! He done made me drap dat chicken. Now whutchu gwine do?" she demanded as John came up too late to help.

John the Baptist was in the full flush of early manhood. He came of kingly stock—Plymouth Rock—and his lordly bearing showed it. Almost from the time he had cracked his shell, he had known no other mother than John. For months and months they had been inseparable, and John the Boy had turned over everything on the place except the house looking for bugs and worms for John the Baptist.

When the rooster's first feathers came, John was playing with him one day near the dairy and Aunt Betsey asked, "Whutchu gwi name dat chicken, Baby?" And without waiting for a reply she continued solemnly, " 'His name is John.' Dat's in de Bible, en John wuz de bigges' en de bes' uv all Chris's 'ciples 'ca'se he wuz a Baptis'. Hit's a good name, Baby, en hit's yo'n, too, so us'll ha' t' call him John." Leaving him wondering if there wasn't some other name he would like better, she went into the kitchen and a minute or two later appeared at the window. "Hyere, Baby," she called, "Gi' dis bread t' John; he sho is gwi be a mighty fine chicken, he is."

That settled it—from that time on his name *was* John. All his life he had showed scant respect for anything or anybody, and as soon as his feathers began to grow he took upon himself the protection of all chickendom. When a chicken was to be killed, he would attack the executioner every time. "Henry Po'ter" was the cause of this. When Henry came to stay at the yard, John the Baptist was just about frying-size; and one day Henry said to John, "Ah tell you whut us do, le's us gi' dat John chicken some gunpowder t' eat, en den he ain' gwi be skeered uv nothin'."

"Whut you wan' t' give 'im dat for?" asked John.

"T' make 'im fight. You ha' t' do dat ef you wan' t' make 'im fight."

"I don't want him t' fight, Henry," said John.

"Howcome you don't? Co'se you do. Ef he don' fight, jes aire one uv dese li'l ole chickens 'll jes run 'im all over de yard. You don' wan' dat—now does you? *Does* you?"

John didn't, but he said "Naw" doubtfully, and he insisted that "eatin' powder didn' do no good."

"Whutchu talkin' 'bout, fel-ler? Co'se hit do's good. Folks is all de time gi'n' dey dawgs powder t' make 'em bad, ain' dey? You know dat. Well howcome hit don' do no good, den? You know hit do."

"But John ain' no *d-o-g,* Henry, he's a *chicken,*" said John very emphatically.

"Whut diff'unce do dat make?" demanded Henry. "He fights, don't he? He got spurs, ain't he? How you reggin he gwi fight a-tall ef he don' ha' sump'm t' make 'im fight? How he gwi do dat, now?"

"Y-e-a-h!" John was derisive. "An' spose us give him some powder en he turn roun' an die? Jus' sposin' dat, now. Den whutchu goin' say?"

"Now jes listen t' you, feller—jes listen t' yo'se'f. You's wuss'n ole Unc' Crazy Pete, you is. He's plum crazy, he is, en he lose all his sense eve'y time de moon change, en he won' listen t' nobody. You's jes lak 'im, you is, en Um gwi call you Unc' Pete f'um dis on. Pete—Pete—Peter! Yeah, dat's hit—Peter!" And he began to chant contemptuously:

> "Peter, Peter, Punkin eater,
> Had a wife en couldn' keep 'er,
> He put 'er in a punkin-shell,
> En den he kep' 'er ve'y well.

Dat's you, en Um gwi call you Peter!"

The fight that followed was one-sided. John couldn't catch Henry, who kept just out of reach and threw back over his shoulder, tauntingly:

"Peter, Peter, Punkin eater." And to Henry, John was always "Peter" after that.

Henry went for the cows alone that evening, but differences were soon forgotten. He and John together fed John the Baptist that night, and John the Baptist's supper was well seasoned with gunpowder.

As a result either of the gunpowder treatment or of natural pugnacity John the Baptist would fight. He would fight not only dogs or chickens or turkeys, but he would fight folks as well. And he had just made Aunt Betsey drop a chicken she was going to kill for dinner.

"Now whutchu gwi do?' she asked John angrily.

John began making excuses for John the Baptist. "He don' know no better, Ai' Betsey," he said pleadingly.

But she was not to be appeased so easily. "He don't, huh? Well, a-l-l right 'bout dat, den; but howcome you ain' come quick when Ah fus' call you? Howcome dat?"

"I did come, Ai' Betsey," John said positively. "I come jus' as quick as—"

"Yeah," she interrupted, "Ah knows you did. You come, but-chu manage mighty well t'gitchere too late jes lak you allus do w'en dat ole *devul* chicken git atter me. Nemmine, us's got t' ha' chicken fer dinner en d'ain't narry nudder'n in de coop; so us'll jes ha' t' kill John de Baptis'; he ain' fittin fer nothin' ilse nohow."

"Naw, you ain't!" The boy held John the Baptist in his arms and looked defiantly over his head at Aunt Betsey. "Naw, you ain't goin' to kill John, Ai' Betsey. You know you ain't," and he hugged the rooster tighter.

"Us ain't, ain't us?" Aunt Betsey asked ominously. "Le's see ef us ain't," and she went to the house.

Still holding his rooster in both arms, John hurried to the cow lot to hide. Then, in search of greater safety he dodged into the wilds of the pea-patch, and there they stayed until another chicken had been caught and killed.

As soon as John the Baptist had definitely established his kingship over the rest of the flock, he whipped a turkey-hen and took three of her young turkeys from her. They were about as large as frying-size chickens then. He hovered them and fed and loved them better than their own mother had done. However, they refused to follow him into the house to roost on the steps; so he carried them to the dairy and under that they slept—one under each wing and one between his legs—until they were as big as he. Then they deserted him to roost in the trees. John the Baptist promptly showed his indifference to this desertion by annexing two young hens and bringing them to roost on the stairway in the back hall.

Nothing much was said about this until Grandma found chicken-mites on the stairway. Then Uncle John spoke: "Make that chicken stay in the henhouse where it belongs or I'm going to eat him, suh!"

John appealed to Auntie but got no help there. She liked John the Baptist but not the chicken-mites. It was no use to ask Grandma to intercede; she had started this trouble in the first place. So he went to Aunt Betsey.

"I don' see howcome they so skeered uv a few little ole chicken-mites, Ai' Betsey," he said. "They don't hu'tchu none, nohow; jus' crawl on you a little. An' 'sides that," he went on with a deepening sense of injury, "'sides that, it ain't right t' make John de Baptis' stay out there in 'at ole henhouse with them ole chickens. You know it ain't, Ai' Betsey. Now is it?"

"Well, Baby, Ah wouldn' say hit 'uz jes zac'ly right, Ah wouldn'—Ah sho wouldn'; 'ca'se dar is jes ez much diff'unce 'twixt John de Baptis' en dem chickens ez d'is 'twixt house-niggers en fiel'-niggers, en dat's de trufe. But dey ha' t' mix up sometimes when dey cain' he'p deyse'fs, en chickens is jes lak dat too. Jes de same," she continued consolingly, "de ve'y fus' thing John gwi do *eve'y* mo'nin' is come up hyere t'see you en git 'is breakfus', en ef us gi' 'im a li'l mo' t' eat en pay 'im jes a li'l mo' 'tention, he ain' gwi nevuh soshate wid dem ole henhouse chickens no mo' en whut he ought t'. Now you see ef Ah ain' right."

With this rather meager comfort, little John had to be satisfied.

FISHIN'

One of John's greatest pleasures was to go with Henry, morning and evening, to drive the cows to and from the pasture.

On the way he would cram his pockets with grasshoppers for John the Baptist, who, though a dignified husband of many wives, would always meet John at the gate and peck his toes if he wasn't fed at once.

This morning John had filled his pockets on the way down, and when they got to the "big hole" in the creek near the pasture gate, Henry suggested that they throw in the grasshoppers to see them swim.

"Naw, I ain't, either. John's got t' have these."

"Us'll ketch plenty mo' fer him," promised Henry. "Come on, Peter, en th'ow 'em in," he wheedled.

"Naw, I ain't, Henry. I ain't a-goin' t' do it, I tell you! I had t' work hard t' ketch 'ese hoppergrasses, an' 'sides 'at, I got t' give'm t' John de Baptis'. If I don't do that he'll be mad wit' me an' you know he will, too."

"Aw fel-ler, s-h-u-ck-s! You all de time thinkin' 'bout dat ole John rooster en you ain' nevuh thinkin' 'bout whut Ah does fer you," said Henry, accusingly. "Didn' Ah he'p you ketch a heap uv 'em yistiddy?" he went on. "En ain' Ah gwi he'p you ketch a heap mo' t'day? You know Um is. So howcome it is you won' th'ow none uv 'em in w'en Ah wants you to? Come on, Peter, en th'ow 'em in."

But John was obstinate. John the Baptist's claims were greater than those of gratitude. He shook his head.

"You ain' gwi do dat, huh?" asked Henry. "You sho is a staingy li'l ole white boy, Peter, you sho is dat. Ah didn' think you 'uz dat staingy. Ah wouldn' be ez staingy ez whut chu is not fer nothin'. Ah sho wouldn'."

"But, Henry, it took me a long time—"

"Naw hit d-i-d-n', Pe-ter, you know hit didn'. Ah tell you whutchu do, den: you th'ow in jes *one*. Don't th'ow 'im too fur en he'll come back dis way, en Ah'll git down hyere by de aige uv de watter en ketch 'im w'en he come out, en den us'll th'ow 'im back ag'in. You gwi do dat, ain'chu, ain'chu now, Peter? You is, ain'chu?"

John relented. "All right, den, I'll th'ow in dis li'l un."

"Naw, now, naw, naw, th'ow in a big 'un, Peter, 'ca'se dey kin swim a heap de bestes'. En 'sides dat, Ah done tole you Um gwi ketch 'im, ain't Ah? He cain' git away nohow wid me right hyere waitin' fer 'im, kin 'e? Den whutchu skeered fer? Come on, Peter, en th'ow 'im in."

So in went a big one, but Henry didn't catch it; for it had hardly started swimming when up came a big school of fish of all sizes, from as big as your hand on down, and before the boys realized it the grasshopper was gone!

"G-r-e-a-t L-a-w-d-y, P-e-t-e-r-r-uh! D'ju see dat? Didju see dat? Dem's goggle-eyes, feller, en eve'y udder kin' uv pyetch dey is in de worl'! Oh my Lawd, dis hole is jes plum full uv fishes! Th'ow in de res' uv dem hoppergrasses, feller!"

The boys were charged with excitement now. In the grasshoppers went—one at a time, and then the boys caught more—not for John the Baptist, but for the fish.

After a bit, Henry suddenly snapped out viciously at John, "Quit dat th'owin' dem things in dar, Peter! You ain' got a bit a sense."

"W'y, Henry," answered John indignantly, "you *tole* me—"

"Dat wuz befo'. Don'chu know us got t' keep 'em hongry so dey'll bite w'en us come fishin' dis e'nin'? Come on now en le's go ax Mars John t' git us some hooks."

Uncle John gave them money for the hooks and let them ride a mule to the store after them. The storekeeper wanted them to get the light, strong lines they needed, but—"No, suh," that wouldn't do. They had to have *big* lines—big enough to hold a cow, even—because there wasn't any telling how big these fish were, and the boys weren't going to take any chances on losing them.

At home, Miss Sallie said "No." She was afraid John would get hurt. Mars John said, "Aw, Sallie," and smiled a promise at John. John said, "Aw shucks, Auntie," and looked at her pleadingly. Then Grandma said she was afraid he'd get wet and catch cold; and Miss Sallie said she was afraid he'd stick a hook in his finger and drown. Aunt Betsey said "Humph!" and waited on the outer edge of the group.

When John, almost in tears, said that they couldn't know how "bad" he wanted to go "'cause Auntie and Grandma never wuz no little boy" like him, Aunt Betsey laughed and said, "He's tellin' you de trufe now, Miss Sallie. En you cain' keep 'im a baby all de time, you cain't," and then she went to the kitchen. Uncle John laughed and said, "Let him go"; he wasn't going to have "no gal-boy" around him, and he got on his horse and rode away. Grandma said "Well," resignedly and went to her room; Auntie said "W-e-l-l," uncertainly, and the boys ran off before she could change her mind. Thus began a whole long summer's fishing.

John refused to spit on his bait before he threw his hook into the water, and Henry said, "Nemmine, you jes don' do it. Go on en be hard-haided, Peter. You won' nevuh listen t' whut nobody tells you, you won't. So jes you go on en don' do it now, en Ah boun'ju you gwi see Um gwi ketch de mo'es' fishes eve'y day. You see ef Ah don't."

When they counted the fish that night, Henry had three more than John. "You see dar now, don'chu?" he asked. John did see, and never afterwards did his hook go into the water unless it carried a generous supply of spit "for luck."

SWIMMIN'

Peter, le's go swimmin'." The fish were biting poorly that afternoon, and the boys were hot and tired.

"Uch-Ur-oh, Auntie wouldn' like it, Henry."

"How you know she wouldn'?" Henry asked almost belligerently.

"I know 'cause she said fer me to be *sho* not to git wet," answered John, "an' you *know* you can't swim wit'out gittin' wet. That's how I know it."

"She ain' mean yo' *skin,* Peter, she mean yo' clo's." Henry was insistent. "Ef she mean yo' skin, howcome she let you go barefeeted en don' nevuh say nothin' 'bout how much you wades in de watter en de mud, too? Howcome dat, now?" he demanded.

"Well, I'll ast her t'night then," said John, anxious to be on the safe side.

"Naw, Peter, don'chu do dat. You listen t' me now, ha' some sense *dis* time en listen t' me. Ef you axes 'er, you mos' know she gwi say Naw, ain't she?"

"Yeah, an' 'at's de reason I'm skeered t' go in, Henry."

"You wait now, feller. Now ef you axes 'er en she say Naw, en den you goes in anyhow, you done done sump'm dat she tole you not to. Ain'chu?"

"Yeah. But—"

"En ef she ax you ef you been in swimmin'," Henry interrupted, "en you say Naw, den you done tole her a story, ain'chu?"

"Yeah, Henry, an' 'at's a sin, too," said John, righteously. "You know Ah ain' goin' t' do dat."

"Ah knows you ain't, Peter, 'ca'se d'ain't gwi be no nuse to. Now," he went on, "ef you don' ax Miss Sallie nothin' 'bout it, she cain' say Naw, kin she?"

John shook his head again.

"En ef you goes in en she ain' say not to, den you ain' done nothin' she tole you not t' do, is you?"

John shook his head again.

"Well, den, ef you goes in en she ain' tole you *not* to, en you don' tell 'er 'bout it t'night so she cain' ax you nothin' 'bout it, den you ain' done nothin' she done tol you not t' do, en you ain' tole 'er no story, en you ain' 'mitted no sin, needer. Now Um's right, ain't Ah, Peter? Ain't Ah, now? Dat's jes ez plain ez day, ain't it?"

The light of understanding broke on John. The water was cool; they were hot and sweaty. Henry said invitingly, "Le's go, Peter," and in they went.

The water was just over waist-deep and cool; so what mattered it that the oozy mud came half-way to their knees? They were happy.

After a while John got tired of just wading and tried to swim like Henry. He pushed with one foot on the bottom and splashed with his hands and remaining foot. Of course, he came to grief. He got his eyes and his ears and his nose and his mouth full of water and had to quit.

That night when the boys were cleaning the fish on the milk table at the dairy and getting scales all over it, Henry handed John the "swimming bladder" from the biggest fish. "Hyere, Peter," he said, "grease dis en swollit."

"Whut fer?" asked the startled John.

"So you kin swim, feller. Ain'chu got no sense?"

"Is you plum crazy, Henry Po'ter?" John demanded indignantly. "Whut I wan' t' swallow 'at ole nasty, raw fishbladder fer? You ain't got no sense yo'se'f, you ain't!"

"My Lawd, Peter! Don'chu know you ha' t' do dat ef you ever is t' l'arn how t' swim? Eve'ybody else ha' t' do dat 'fo' dey kin swim; so how you spec' you gwi l'arn les'n you does it, too? How you spec' dat? *You* ain' no fish; you ain' got no swimmin' bladder; so how you spec's t' git aire un les'n you swollit?"

John backed off and Henry followed, holding out the bladder invitingly. "Hyere, Peter," he said firmly, *"swollit."*

"I ain't goin' t' do it, I tell you, Henry," John almost screamed at him. "How you spec' me t' swallow 'at ole nasty, bloody thing an' it's big ez a puck-cawn, too?"

"Don' kyere how big hit is, Peter, you kin swollit," insisted Henry. "You could swolly a hawg bladder ef hit 'uz gwi keep you f'um drowndin', en you know you could! So you jes ez well come on en swollit right now," he said with determination.

"I ain't! I ain't, I tell you!" John was equally determined. "How you know whut good'll it do?" he demanded. "How you know hit'll make me swim? How you know dat, now?"

"Dar you go ag'in, Peter," said Henry, disgustedly, "Dar you go. You en ole Unc' Crazy Pete's jes alak. Won' narry one uv you nevuh b'lieve nothin' whut nobody tells you. You all de time axin' how Ah knows sump'm gwi do good. Don't Ah know hit do's good? En ain't Um tellin' you? Whut mo' you want? Ef you don' b'lieves me, you ax Ai' Betsey; ax Net; ax Ai' Em'ly; ax Unc' Harry; ax anybody whut's got any sense en dey'll tell you eve'ybody ha' t' do dat 'fo' dey kin swim." He lowered his voice and continued, "En Um gwi tell you dis: Ah ain' gwine in swimmin' wid you no mo' les'n you *do* swollit."

"Howcome you ain't?" asked John, lowering his voice also and looking around cautiously.

"Howcome? Dar you go ag'in, Peter! Howcome? Howcome?" he quoted derisively, "Hit's 'howcome dis?' en 'Howcome dat?' all de time wid you, ole Unc' Pete. Dat's de way hit is. Sposin' you go swimmin' en gits drownded, whutchu gwi say den? You'll wush you had swollit dat bladder den, wouldn'chu? En Miss Sallie en Mars John 'ud be mad wid me when hit wouldn' be my fault a-tall, but jes *you*, 'ca'se you's ackin' lak a ole mule. You lak t' got strangle' t' death dis e'nin', you know you did; en Ah jes ain' gwine in wid you no mo', Peter, les'n you does swollit. Ah jes cain' ris' it."

"I'm goin' t' ast Ai' Betsey," said John referring to his fountainhead of all knowledge.

"All right, den, ax 'er. Dar she in de kitchen," said Henry, pointing, "Ax 'er, en Ah boun'ju she gwi say you ha' t' do it, too. You see ef she don't."

John called Aunt Betsey to the kitchen window. "Ai' Betsey," he said, "Henry Po'ter wants t' make me swallow a nasty ole fish bladder, 'cause he say I can't never learn how t' swim if I don't do it. Dat don't do no good, do it?"

Aunt Betsey smiled at first; but when she answered, her voice and her eyes were serious. "Oh yes, hit do do's good, Honey," she said. "Ah been hyeahin' dat *all my life*. All de ole folks'll tell you dat."

"How can 'at do any good, Ai' Betsey?" asked John.

"Well, Baby, dar's a heap a things us jes cain' zac'ly un'erstan', but us knows dey *is* so, anyhow. Ah spec', dough, hit's dissaway. Folks jes nach'ly ain' got no swimmin' bladder, 'ca'se ef dey did have dey'd be jes ez much at home in de watter ez dey is on de groun'. You know dat. So ef dey wan' t' swim, dey fus' ha' t' git a bladder f'um a fish 'ca'se dat's de only sump'm whut's got one; en de onliest way dey kin git it in dey belly whar it 'longst t' be is t' swollit. You run along now, Baby, en swollit. Hit ain't gwi hu'tchu, hit's gwi do you good."

So John went back to Henry, eager now to get it over with. Henry in the meantime had found another bladder, and holding it up he said, "Peter, jes to show you— But whut Ai' Betsey say?" he asked suddenly.

"She say swollit," answered John.

"You see dar now? Ah tole you she 'uz gwi say do it!" jubilantly exclaimed Henry. "But jes to show you Ah ain't tellin' you nothin' wrong," he went on, "when you swolly yo'n, Um gwi swolly dis'n. Dat's fair 'nough fer anybody, ain't it?"

"All right, den," agreed John, "but gimme a li'l un, Henry. That'n's too big."

"Naw, Peter, you swolly dis'n. Ef you swolly a li'l un, you'll jes swim lak a li'l ole pyetch or a topwater. Swolly a big un, feller, so you kin swim lak a *big* fish!"

"It'll choke me, Henry," objected John. "It's too big."

"*Naw* hit ain't, Peter, naw hit ain't. Us'll grease 'em good en you'll see dey gwi slip down yo' th'oat 'fo' you knows it."

"You swallow yo's fus', den, Henry." John was afraid Henry would back out.

"Naw, Peter, you go fus', now."

"Naw, Henry, you go fus'," John insisted. All the salty bacon grease in the world couldn't make that bloody bladder palatable.

"Ah tell you whut us do, den, Peter. Us swollem t'gedder! You count, en us'll see which'n gits his'n down de fustes'. Dat's fair, now ain't it?"

John agreed. They opened their mouths wide, and, to insure an even start, held the bladders as close to them as they could. John counted:

> "*One* fer de money,
> *Two* fer de show,
> *Three* t' make ready,
> An' *four* fer t' go!"

And down they went.

THE FUNERAL OF THE SINFUL CHICKEN

Whenever one of the chickens died in the yard, it was John's and Henry Porter's job to bury it. These interments also included cats and pups—in fact, anything they could handle. Burials soon flourished into funerals—big funerals at which the boys took turn about in the preaching, while John's small sister and five or six little negroes from the quarters made up the congregation and mourners.

One morning a chicken, almost frying-size, was found dead under the dairy, and Henry woke John with—"Peter, git up, feller! Us got a fune'l t' preach dis mo'nin'."

"Who daid?" asked John, instantly awake.

"One dem nigh half-growed chickens whut roos' un'er de dairy. Ah done fixt de watter fer you t' wash yo' face. Huh'y up, feller! Us got a h-e-a-p t' do."

"Whut?"

"Well fus', us got t' take de cows t' de paster. Won' ha' time t' beh'y 'im 'fo' dat, 'ca'se dis's got t' be a *big* fune'l. (Button up dat wais' w'ile you comin' en come on en wash yo' face. You sho is slow dis mo'nin'.) Den atter us git back," he continued, "us got t' make de coffin en de haid-bo'ds en dig de grave en git word to all de folkses. So you see us gwi be busy. Hyere, wipe yo' face now—you done wash enough. Come on, breakfus' mos' ready."

"Wait a minute, Henry, I got to comb my hair."

"Aw comb it terreckly; Ah wan' t' show you dat co'pse 'fo' de breakfus' bell ring."

But Uncle John was already in the dining room and he sang out: "Run comb that head *now*, son. Breakfast will be ready right away and you mustn't keep us waiting." He wanted everybody present when the blessing was asked. Henry followed upstairs to Ole Mistis' room. "Now you see dar, don'chu? Ef you had'n wash so much en talk so much, Ah'd a showed you dat—." Then a new thought struck him. "Lawd, Lawd, Lawd! Ah sho is glad Ah don' ha' t' comb my haid eve'y time Ah wash *my* face."

"Shucks! You ain't got nothin' to comb."

"Yeah, en dat's 'ca'se Ah's got sense. Mammy nuseter cyard it eve'y two weeks; en w'en she git th'ough, my haid 'ud be

so'e twel time t' cyard it ag'in. But las' week Ah gi'n Unc'
Harry a big chaw uv 'bac'er whut Marse John gi'n me, en he
tuck de mule shears en cut it close off jes lak you see hit now.
Hope t' Gawd hit don' *nevuh* grow out no mo'. Dar de bell!"
On the way to the dining room he confided: "Las' night Miss
Sallie tole Net she gwi make me l'arn t' wait on de table. Ah
don' kyere, dough, 'ca'se she say Ah got t' ha' some new shu'ts
en anudder pa'r uv britches fus' en Ah betchu Ah gits Miss
Sallie's plate eve'y time. Y'see 'fah don't!"

Breakfast was soon over. They fed John the Baptist the bis-
cuit crusts saved for him, and gave the kittens fresh milk
begged from "Ai' Em'ly." Before they left for the pasture, Henry
got a shingle; and on that for a "coolin'-bo'd" the corpse was
laid to await further preparation. John wanted to leave it on
the milk table at the dairy—"out of the way of those mean old
cats that eat dead folks," but "Ai' Em'ly" firmly vetoed that
plan. "Naw-s-u-h, Baby, you cain' leave 'im dar."

"He won't hurt nothin', Ai' Em'ly," John pleaded.

"Nunch, nunch. Cain' do dat, 'ca'se eve'y one uv dem cows
'ud git de milk fever ef a dead chicken wuz lef' roun' dey
milk. Maybe die, too, en Ah know you don' wan' yo' Polly
cow t' do dat, now does you?"

John didn't want that, of course, but still he pointed out
that the chicken wasn't on the table really, but on the "coolin'-
bo'd."

Aunt Emily chuckled out loud. It was a throaty sort of
sound that made you want to hold to her dress, for it sounded
like a caress. "L-a-w-d G-a-w-d have mussey on dese chillun!
Sis Betsey," she called to the kitchen, "d'you hyeah whut dese
chillun doin' now? Got dis ole chicken laid out on a coolin'-
bo'd. Why, Honey," she said, turning to John, "hit's col'
a'ready—he plum stiff. You don' need no coolin'-bo'd fer him."

"Yes us do, Ai' Emily," he said, beginning to dance around
her, delighted at the interest she was showing, "Yes us do,

'cause us goin' t' have a *big* funeral this time en you can't have no big funeral widout no coolin'-bo'd. Ken you, Henry?"

Loyal support from Henry was not lacking; so Aunt Emily said, "Ah tell you whut you ought t' do—git one uv de kitchen cheers en lay 'im on dat. Dat'll be mo' lak it. En put 'im out un'er dat big tree in de shade, too, Baby. Don' leave 'im clost roun' hyere 'ca'se de flies be too bad."

John got two chairs and across these the shingle cooling-board was left while the boys took the cows to the pasture. They got there in record time.

On the way back Henry stopped to chase an enormous butterfly. When he caught it, he held it out to John with, "Yere Peter, bite 'is haid off quick, en you gwi git a new suit a clo's."

"Whut fer?" John asked, startled.

"Do dat en you git you a new suit a clo's."

"I don't want no mo' clo's, Henry." John didn't care to bite.

"Now jes listen t' dat! Jes listen now! Co'se you want some mo' clo's. Ah had two pa'r britches en three shu'ts, didn' Ah? Well, Sa'day 'fo' dis las' un gone, Ah bit one's haid off jes lak dis'n, en now look whut hap'm. Gwi git two shu'ts en some mo' britches. D'you see?"

But John was still skeptical. "Yeah, an' one of them britches you got is tore all up an' a shirt too, an—"

"Don' kyere ef dey is, Ah still got 'em, ain't ah? En now Um gittin' some mo'. Go on, Peter," he coaxed, "en bite it."

"All right," but John hesitated further. "How do I know yo' clo's come from that?"

"Well now jes hyeah dat, will you! Jes listen! Don' Ah know how Ah git dem clo's, en ain't Um tellin' you? En Ah ai' nevuh tell you wrong, is Ah now, is Ah? You sho is hard-haided, P-e-ter." Henry's disgust at such ignorance and unbe-lief showed in his voice. "Now," he snapped, "bite it off quick, feller, 'ca'se us got t' go t' dat fune'l!"

John bit! As soon as it was done and before he was through scraping the remains of the butterfly's head off his tongue with a muddy forefinger, Henry was jumping up and down with delight! "Gwi git some mo' clo's! Peter gwi git some mo' clo's! Hot-chu, feller! Us gwi dress up some Sunday en go t' Mars Stephens t' dinner, en chu'ch, too! *Ain't* us? Huh?"

Now that the clothes had been guaranteed, John wanted to know how soon he could expect them.

"Ah don' know 'bout dat," said Henry. "Hit may be a long time er maybe sooner, but you sho gwi git 'em—you watch!"

When they got home, Aunt Emily had covered the "co'pse" with a nice, white piece of tablecloth, given her for rags, and had laid a May-pop bloom and a rosebud on it. Henry looked at Aunt Emily's floral offering for a minute and said softly, "Now ain't dat p'utty, Peter?"

When the boys suggested making a coffin, Mars John refused to lend them the saw. He had tried them once before; so they had to find a box that would do. John had a cigar box that Henry wanted to use, but—"Naw s-u-h, I can't spare that." It was the only thing he had in which to keep his marbles, star-rocks, shells, snake rattles, and the buckeye he carried fishing for luck and after dark to keep off "ha'nts." They finally decided on a shoe box and painted it black with shoe-blacking.

"Hot dawg!" said Henry, "look at dat, now!" Then they took strings and made handles. The box was lined with an old piece of "cyarpet," and for a shroud they used the "death-sheet," furnished by Aunt Emily. The hearse was a piece of plank about two feet long. A string, tied to a nail driven in one end, served both as tongue and harness. Chuck and Sam, two brothers, and Dick, all favorites from the quarters, having been notified of the impending funeral and asked to tell all "de udder folkses," had sent word that they'd "be dar *sho,* en all de folkses."

Before the congregation arrived, John told Henry that as
this was such a big funeral, he was going to ask Aunt Betsey
for a text. But Henry protested, "Um gwine t' preach dis'n,
ain't Ah?"

"Naw you ain't. You preached the last one."

"Naw Ah didn'."

"You did, Henry! You *know* you did!—'cause the last'n was
that little chicken whut ole Charley horse stepped on. You
preached that'n. You know you did!"

"Don' kyere ef Ah did. Disn' got t' be diff'unt f'um de res',
en you don' know how t' do it."

"Howcome it's diff'unt? A chicken's a chicken, ain't it?"

"Co'se hit's diff'unt, Peter. Some kin' uv folkses has one kin'
uv fune'l en de udder kin' uv folkses has anudder kin'. You
know dat. Well chickens de same way, en dis'n's one uv de
udder kin'."

"Whut kin' mus' I preach, den?"

"Nemmine, nemmine, jes you preach hit en Ah boun'ju you
gwi make a mess uv it. En ef you does, um sho gwine preach
it right."

The congregation being assembled at the home of the deceased—the dairy—nothing was left but the final arrangements
and the funeral. Since John's little sister happened to be the
only girl in the congregation, they told her that she would
have to be "de gal mo'ner." She kicked! She said she wasn't
a girl, but a boy just like John was. She pointed out that she
didn't wear dresses, except Sundays and when company came,
but pants just like he did, and, further, she knew she was a boy
because "Pa" and "Ma" (their Uncle and Aunt) said so. The
boys were up against a snag until they persuaded her to "jes
'ten' lak you'z a ooman—not no gal chile but a grown ooman."
She consented to do this after they had got her a big umbrella
weed to use as a parasol. Sam and Chuck volunteered to

double as mules to pull the hearse and to act as mourners at the cemetery.

So the procession started. When the funeral party arrived at the graveyard, one of the mourners borrowed a shovel from Charley's stable near by, and friends of the deceased dug the grave. The mules were now mourners. The ease and solemnity with which Sam and Chuck assumed their various rôles bespoke rare histrionic ability. After two verses of song, John rose to deliver the sermon.

"Folkses," said he, "this po' little chicken's dead. He sho is dead, folkses." Henry's look of disgust was getting John rattled. "He wuz a good little chicken, folkses, but he dead now an' gone to heaven."

"Ah knowed it! Ah knowed it! Ah tole you so!" The words fairly whistled! "Ah knowed you's gwi do it wrong! Didn' Ah say so? Yes, Ah did!" Henry ended triumphantly.

"'Tain't wrong a-tall," John defended.

"H-u-r-r-huh! h-u-r-r-huh!" Henry laughed derisively. "Co'se hit's wrong Peter. Dat wa'n't no good li'l chicken—hit didn' go t' no heb'm! You ought t' preach 'im down to hell!"

"Howcome I ought t' preach 'im down to hell? Chickens go to chicken-heaven, don't they?"

"N-a-w dey don't! Not all uv 'em do, dey don't. All de folkses don't go to heb'm, do dey? Well, chickens jes de same ez folkses, ain't dey? Dey is," he answered his own question. 'En dis'n 'uz sho one uv dem los' sinners."

"But Henry, how you *know* he wuz one of them sinner chickens?"

"How Ah know? How Ah know? Ain't dat de same chicken you wushed wuz daid de udder day? En didn' you run at 'im en try t' kill 'im en pull mos' all 'is tail out w'en he fit dat po' li'l sickly baby chicken whutchu wuz feedin'? En dat li'l sickly chicken died too, didn' 'e? Ef you don' b'lieve dat's de same ole mean chicken, you jes op'm dat coffin en see ef mos' all uv 'is tail ain' gone en two uv 'is whing fedders wuz broke, too. Now whut you say?"

"How us know he didn' 'pent, Henry, jes 'fo' he died?"

"Ain't n-o-body hyeahd 'im, is dey? En ef he'd a 'pented somebody would a been boun' t' hyeahd 'im, wouldn' dey? Co'se he didn' 'pent, Peter, en he got t' go t' hell, too. 'Ez de tree fall, so shell hit lie.' Dat's in de Bible—you know dat, en ef you don't, hit's dar jes de same. Dat's so, ain't it, Chuck? Ain't it, Sam?" The whole congregation nodded their heads. With defeat staring him in the face, John's eyes filled with tears. He was particularly anxious for that chicken to go to heaven on account of those tail feathers. When Henry saw the tears, he softened a little—"Aw, shucks, Peter, don'chu cry." Then, brightly—"Yes, you do! You cry, Peter, en you make de bes' kin' uv mo'ner. Cry, feller! Hot-dawg! Sing anudder vus uv dat song, folkses, w'ile de haid mo'ner git chuned up good." John did his duty, and in a minute or two "de ooman mo'ner" was helping him.

Henry pulled an almanac from his pocket, and in Brother Shadrach Thompson's most unctious voice he began: "Brethren en Sisters, Ah takes my tex' f'um dat part uv de Bible whut say, 'Hell is fer sinners, en ef you once git in you cain' *nevuh* git out.'" After a slight impressive pause he continued, "Dat's in de Bible, folkses, en us knows, us does, dat hit's de trufe." His voice suddenly changed to a singsong tone, and he punctuated each sentence with a short, sharp "Hah!"

"W'en you once gits in, you cain' n-e-v-u-h git out, hah! W'en de chillun uv Gawd di-ees dey g-o-e-s to heb'm, hah! Dey g-o-e-s to Glory, hah! W'en a sinner di-ees dey goes to de devul, hah! Dey g-o-e-s to hell, hah! Dis po' li'l chicken, hah! He wuz a sinner, hah! He's gone to hell, hah! He wouldn' 'pent, hah! Us tried to git 'im to 'pent, hah! Us ax 'im to pray, hah! He wouldn' do it, hah! He tole his mammy lies, hah! He steal de udder chickens' vittles, hah! He fit all de li'l sickly chickens, hah! Now de devul's got 'im, hah! In a red-hot chicken coop, hah! Hit's made out uv i-yun, hah! He cain' git out, hah! Ur-r-r-h *sinner*, you got to 'pent 'fo' you dies, hah! 'Ca'se you c-a-i-n' 'pent atterwu'ds, hah! Ur-r-r-r-h chick-e-n-n, hah! Hit's too late now, hah! Don' b-e-g Aberham, hah! t' fetch you no watter, hah! He c-a-i-n' reach you-u-u-oo, hah! De fiah's hot, hah! Hit's made out'n san', hah! De Jaybird fetch it, hah! Eve'y Friday, hah! Ur-r-r-h J-a-y-bird, Jaybird, fetch on mo' san', hah! De Devul's dar, hah! Wid a red-hot pitchfock, hah! He punch dat chicken, hah! He burn off 'is fedders, hah! He burn off his toes, hah! He burn off his eyes, hah! Dey grow out ag'in, hah! He burn 'em some mo', hah! Dat chicken beg, hah! U-r-r Mister Devul, p-l-e-a-s-e suh, le'me 'lone, hah! Ur-r-r-r-uh chick-e-n-n-n, chick-en, chicken, you cain' 'pent now, hah!—Brer Sam, lead us in prayer."

"Hol' on, Brer Henry," objected Chuck, "Brer Sam prayed at de las' fune'l. Hit's my time t' pray now."

"Dat is so," agreed Henry, "Brer Chuck, you lead us in prayer. Moan 'im 'long, folkses, en he'p 'im."

Now Chuck had also sat in church under Brother Shadrach Thompson, and he chanted in a most pious voice a rhythmic prayer, every sentence accented by an explosive popping of his hands.

All the congregation began a low moaning wail, and to that as an accompaniment Chuck prayed: "Ur-r-r-r L-awd (pop!), dis po' li'l chicken done daid en gone to hell (pop!). Ur-r-r-r-oo Lawd, he wouldn' 'pent w'ile he wuz on dis ye'th en he c-a-i-n' 'pent now (pop!). Ur-r-r-r-h Lawd, dey's a heap mo' folkses on dis ye'th jes lak whut dis chicken wuz, en w'en dey dies de good Chris'chuns got to preach dem down to hell jes lak us done done dis sinner (pop!). Ur-r-r-r Lawd, keep de good folkses good so de devul cain' git 'em (pop!). M-a-k-e de sin-ners 'pent so de devul cain' git 'em (pop!). En ef dey j-e-s won' 'pent w'ile dey is on dis ye'th, Lawd, you put 'em down in dat red-hot chicken coop wid dis p-o-o-o' sinner whut j-e-s gone. A-a-a-aman."

"A-a-a-man," responded the congregation, and then Henry rose and "lined out" a hymn—two lines at a time:

"Am I bawn to die, to lay dis body down,
  En shell my trem'lin' soul arise en wear a starry crown?
  Shell I be cah'ed to de skies on flow'ry beds uv ease,
  Whilest udders fit to win de prize en sail th'ough bloody
    seas?"

They had filled the grave and were ready to put in the "haid-bo'ds" when Aunt Betsey called out: "You Baby—you Henry! All you chillun come 'ere."

"Us busy, Ai' Betsey."

"All right den, all right. Jes stay dar en Ah boun'ju Um gwi th'ow eve'y bit a dis watterme'm t' Sis Jane's hawgs!" And she started toward the fence with a watermelon in her arms. No grief under the sun could stand that threat. The mourners left the cemetery with a whoop—"de ooman mo'ner," parasol forgotten, in the lead.

After the melon feast, they decided it was too late to put in the "haid-bo'ds"; so they saved them for the next funeral.

"WHO KILLED COCK ROBIN?"

Dar, Honey, eat *all* uv dat yo'se'f." Aunt Betsey was smiling as she set a great big dish in front of John, but she was in earnest too. On the dish were brains—a whole set of brains—the brains of one lone robin!

It was John's ninth birthday, and Uncle John had listened to his pleas to be allowed to shoot a "big gun jus' once." A fat robin on the table was the result. Uncle John had wanted to hold the gun and let him pull the trigger, but that didn't suit little John—of course not; that would do for "li'l chillun," but he was nine years old today and *big*. Hadn't Aunt Betsey and Uncle Alford both told him that soon—in a year or two at most—he'd be as big a man as Uncle John was; hadn't Uncle Alford said last Sunday that when little John put on Mars John's shoes and walked around in the hall that "f'um de soun' uv his foots he couldn' tell 'im f'um Mars John his-se'f?" Uncle John knew all this, because John had told him. Now he wanted to hold the gun for John and just let him pull the trigger. Didn't nobody hold the gun for Uncle John when he shot it the first time, and he killed a yellow-hammer, too.

So Uncle John said "all right," and then Auntie said "No." She was afraid the gun might kick John. This started a three-cornered argument—John and Uncle John on one side and Auntie on the other. Auntie was about to win it, too, when Aunt Betsey, who had been listening and smiling all the while, said, "Dat gun ain't gwi hu't dat boy, Miss Sallie, Mars John'll see t' dat. Le' 'im go on en shoot, en ef he do kill aire bird Um's sho gwine cook it fer his supper."

Miss Sallie gave in. Aunt Betsey pulled a pin from something red that hung from her neck inside her dress and, with a whispered "Dis is yo' luck-pin," stuck it in John's waist. Uncle John loaded the gun—one barrel, cocked it, and handed it to John, saying, "Hold it up, suh, and be careful."

John walked to the yard fence. High up in an oak near by was one lone robin. Aunt Betsey and Miss Sallie held their fingers in their ears while John took a long and careful aim. B-O-O-M! He staggered back from the blow against his shoulder and knew he had been kicked. But when, through the hazy black powder smoke, he saw the robin tumble to the ground, he forgot the recoil of the gun—it didn't hurt much, anyway.

Uncle John exclaimed, "Bully for you, suh!" Auntie said, "He *did* do it!" Later she put the feathers carefully away in a box and wrote John's name and the date on it. Aunt Betsey felt the red charm in the bosom of her dress and said, "Huh! Ah knowed he 'uz gwi do it"; and when in the kitchen Uncle Alford asked John if he wasn't going to divide that bird with him, she nearly snapped his head off.

"Naw!" she shouted at him. "Naw, he ain't, you greedy-gutted ole fool! He gwine eat eve'y speck uv dat bird hisse'f."

At supper that night the robin was put on a little saucer by John's plate, but the brains—that one set of robin's brains—was served alone on a great big dish—a dish so big he could scarcely reach over it. Aunt Betsey explained that eating the brains of his first kill would make him always smarter than the game, and that the big dish showed the size of his future kills.

There must have been something to this, for in after years John filled that dish many, many times.

WARTS AND OTHER THINGS

John was playing alone in the back yard but without much success, for Henry was away on an errand. Aunt Betsey came out of the kitchen with a basket on her arm.

"Baby," she called, "whutchu doin'?"

"Playin'."

"Playin' whut?"

"I ain't playin' nothin', Ai' Betsey, I'm waitin' fer Henry Po'ter t' come back. He gone to take the clothes to Ai' Calline en Auntie wouldn't let me go too."

"Dat's so—dis is Monday en de wash ha' t' go out. Well, Um gwine t' de pea-patch. Wan' t' go wid me?"

The little fellow jumped up. "Yes'm. Le' me tote the basket, Ai' Betsey."

"Tote hit all you wants to, Honey, dar en back ag'in, en atter dat you kin he'p me shell dem peas. Ah needs some he'p t'day anyhow, 'ca'se Ah got a powerful mis'ry in my back, Ah is."

"You reckon you straint it, Ai' Betsey?" John asked anxiously.

"Naw, Honey, hit ain't dat, Ah knows, 'ca'se Ah ain't done nothin' fer t' do dat fer de longes' kin' uv time, Ah ain't. Ah knows whut done it, Ah does. Yistiddy me en Sis Nervy wuz walkin' along en talkin' 'bout gwine t' de baptizin' at San' Creek dis nex' Sunday comin', en Ah step over a track whut a snake made w'en he cross de road. Ah seed it, Ah did, but Ah didn' gi' it no 'tention den 'ca'se us 'uz busy talkin' 'bout dem thutty-one candidates whut got t' be baptize' en dat big preacher, Brer—Brer—Brer sump'm er nuther, Ah fergits 'is name right now, f'um up 'bout Egypt, whut's gwi do de baptizin'. W'en us come back Ah seed dat snake's track ag'in en den Ah 'membered 'bout seein' it de fus' time, but hit 'uz too late den t' do anything. Ah knowed Ah wuz gwi have dat mis'ry in my back—*sho.*"

"Can't you cure it, Ai' Betsey?" he asked.

"Well, Ah could, Honey, ef Ah had some snake-ile linimint. Dat's mighty good, hit is, en Ah's got t' make some. But ef Ah had a jes thought w'en Ah fus' step over dem tracks en had a step back ove'm ag'in back'ards en made a cross mark en den walk roun' it, Ah wouldn' be suff'rin' lak Um is now. De Lawd put 'is signs hyere fer folks to read, en ef you don' do it en min' 'em—you sho gwi suffer fer it."

"Howcome that, Ai' Betsey?" asked John.

"Lawd, Honey, you cain't go th'ough dis worl' widout some sor'rs uv some kin' er anudder. Ah knows dat. Hit's jes nachel fer hit to be dattaway, 'ca'se man is jes nach'ly bawn into de worl' in sor'r en sin, en some suff'rin's you's boun' to have. But mos' uv 'em wouldn' tech us ef us pay 'tention t' dem signs. Now a heap a signs say do dis en do dat en you be aw right. De worl' is jes full uv sperrits, hit is. Some uv 'em is good en some is bad, en de good sperrits is got dey signs en de bad uns got dey'n. Ah don' know howcome de Lawd let it be dis way—hit is, dough. But Ah does know all uv 'em, good en bad, got t' make signs eve'ywhar dey go. He gi' you dat much he'p, en, ef you use 'em, you gwi be a heap better off."

"Do you know all the signs there is, Ai' Betsey?"

"Le' me s-e-e-e. Well, Honey, Ah cain' jes zac'ly say ez how Ah knows all uv'm, 'ca'se dar's a mighty heap uv'm, dey is, en ef you put 'em all t'gedder dey'd make a book mos' big ez de Bible, Ah spec'. So bein' dey is dat many dey's boun' to be one er two er maybe three dat's done slip my 'membrance right now, but not many, dey ain't—naw, not many."

All the while this was going on, they were picking peas at a great rate, and now they had nearly enough. John wanted to know how he could tell signs and know what to do.

"Ast, Honey," she answered impressively, "Ast de ole folks, dey knows. Ef you sees somethin' dat ain't nachel, dat's a sign. *Ef hit ain't nachel, hit's a sign!* You 'member dat. Now de Bible say dat signs wuz putchere fer man t' read. So, ef you cain' do de readin', de nex' bes' thing t' do is t' ast some-body whut kin, en den, do whut dey tells you. Hit's a whole lot mo' safer t' do wrong tryin' t' do right dan hit is t' do wrong not tryin' t' do nothin' a-tall, en you 'member dat, too."

When enough peas were picked, they started back to the house with John in the lead carrying the basket. Soon he spied a little toad. Dropping the basket, he made a dive for the toad and caught it.

"Look, Ai' Betsey," he exclaimed jubilantly, "I caught 'im! Ain't he p'utty?"

"Whut? Dat frawg? Put it down, Honey, *put-tit down!* Ah thought you wuz atter dat butterfly."

But John wanted the toad—insisted on it. It was little and pretty, and besides that, "frogs don't bites you, nohow."

"Ah knows dey don't bites you, Baby; but you put it down anyways, 'ca'se ef he wets on yo' han', hit'll be jes plum full a warts. Ah spec' he done done it now." It had. "Ah thought so. Now you see dar? Wush Ah had some stump-water t' wash yo' han' in, dat 'ud stop 'em 'fo' dey starts. Nemmine, dough, Ah'll fix it w'en us git t' de house."

While she was picking up the peas, John was teasing the toad but not touching it. He was making it jump and jumping with it, jump for jump. Soon he tried to see how close he could jump to the toad without touching it.

"You's gwi kill dat frawg terreckly," Aunt Betsey warned, "en dat's bad luck."

"No'm, I ain't," John answered, but he did. They had jumped together—the frog jumping too far or not far enough, and down came John's bare heel on its back!

"Ah tole you so, Baby, en Ah tole you hit wuz bad luck. You ought t' listen. Now de fus' thing you know you gwi stump de ball uv yo' toe off."

"Howcome, Ai' Betsey?" John was worried now.

"'Ca'se dat's a sign, Honey, en hit's a sign Ah ain't *nevuh* know t' fail. W'en you kills a frawg, you sho gwi stump de ball off'n yo' toe, en dey ain' no mistake 'bout dat."

"But I didn't aim to kill the frog," John protested; "I wasn't even tryin' to hurt it; I was jus' playin' wid it."

"Ah know, Ah know. But you done kill it jes de same. Ah tole you you's gwi do it. Ah warn' you good, Ah did, but you wouldn' listen. C'mon en le's go t' de house. Ah kin fix it so dem warts won' come, but Ah sho cain' he'p dat toe."

At the kitchen the old woman put salt, black pepper, a little sugar, nine drops of turpentine, and a crushed chinaberry leaf in a cup and stirred the mixture thoroughly. "Ah wush Ah had some pokebeh'ies t' put in it, but dis will do," she said as she squeezed some onion juice into the cup. She poured the remedy in a pan of warm water, and John scrubbed his hands vigorously.

"Now you aw right," Aunt Betsey assured him, "Dey ain't comin' now, en ef dey do, us'll git em off anyways."

After a busy silence while they shelled peas, she said, "Ah been thinkin'—" There was a long pause. "Lak Ah said, dar's signs fer eve'ything. Some signs say, 'Do dis en you have good luck.' En some say, 'You gwi do dis.' En ag'in, some say, 'You done done dis, en ef you don' go en do sump'm ilse, you gwi ha' had luck.' But de wustes' signs uv all is dem whut say sump'm lak death er trouble gwi hap'm anyhow, no matter whut you do. You jes ha' t' wait fer dat—wait en pray." Then—"Don' you wuh'y 'bout dem warts," she broke in as John stopped shelling peas to see if any warts were coming. "Ef any uv'm does come, Um gwi take a brass pin en pick it twel hit bleeds, en wrop de blood up in a peachtree leaf en make you th'ow hit over yo' lef' shoulder en walk away widout lookin' back, er ilse beh'y it in de focks uv de road. Ah specs dat'll be de bes', 'ca'se you kin look back den. You know Lot's wife turned into a pillar uv salt w'en she looked back atter dey tole her not to, en ever sence den, w'en folkses looks back w'en dey oughtn' to, bad luck comes foll'in' right behime 'em. En Ah knows, Ah does, hit's mighty hard fer young folks not t' look back. Now, dey is a heap a ways t' take warts off'n you, dey is, but de way Ah jes tole you is ez good ez any, en you got t' l'arn t' let good 'nough alone.

"Aw'ile ago, us 'uz talkin' 'bout backaches en snake-ile linimint en sich. Now, snake-ile is good fer all sorts uv backache en mis'ries in de j'ints, en spesh'ly dem whut a snake put on you. En rattlesnake-ile is de bestes' uv all. De ole folks nuse t' say dat 'uz 'ca'se a rattlesnake wuz de wustes' uv all snakes, en w'en Gawd made 'im, He jes made his ile de bes', so ez t' sorta ekil 'im up. Ah don' know 'bout dat, but you gwi fin' mos' eve'ything is jes dat way—don' kyere how bad hit is, hit's good fer sump'm. Take a black frizzly chicken—Gawd know dey is de devul's own chillun—yit en still, ef you cut one op'm en tie it on a snake-bite, dey ain' nothin' in de worl' dat'll cyore hit any quicker den dat will. You see?

"Now, Um gwi ax you dis—W'en you diggin' baits you ain' think dey's good fer nothin' but ketchin' fishes, is you?"

"No'm," John answered, wonderingly.

"Ah thought so. Well now, you listen t' dis. Ef you take some uv dem baits, de red uns de bes', en rend' de grease out uv'm jes lak you do w'en you makin' lard at hawg-killin' time, den put in a few draps uv te'pentime, a little asfedity en de juice out'n a red ingon, you's got a linimint den dat'll cyore any kin' uv mis'ry er rheumatiz dar is in de worl'. Ef yo' j'ints is swelled up, you kin take some live worms en tie on it, en dat swellin' gwi be gone in no time. De reason uv dat is, worms ain' jes worms, dey's livin' ye'th, en us is too. En dat linimint is jes boun' t' be good 'ca'se man is made out'n ye'th, de pinetree sucks de te'pentime out'n de ye'th, de ingon gits hit's strengt' f'um de ye'th, en Gawd alone knows how deep you ha' t' dig t' git de asfedity out'n de ye'th. So w'en you puts all dese t'gedder, you jes boun' t' git a medicine whut cain't no mis'ry stan' 'g'inst."

"Look, Ai' Betsey," John said suddenly, pointing to the stove. "Sump'm's burning up." Smoke was pouring out of the oven.

"My Gawd'lmighty, ef Ah ain't fergit it!" she exclaimed, jumping up and taking the charred remains of a big sweet potato from the stove. "Now you see dar, Honey, Ah been tellin' 'bout signs en sich ez dat, en done overlook one uv de plaines' dar is. Ah put dat tater in de stove fer you, jes 'fo' us went t' de pea-patch, en w'en Ah tu'n roun' Ah knock a fock off'n de table. Ah ought t' 'membered dat dat means burnt vittles en made a cross mark w'en Ah picked it up, er ilse, th'owed a pinch uv salt in de fiah. Eve'ything would ha' been aw right den, but Ah didn' do it, en now you ain't got no tater. Dat jes proves whut Ah said befo'—signs is putchere fer you t' read, en ef you don' do it—en min' 'em—you sho gwi suffer fer it."

A i’ Betsey,” begged John one afternoon, “sew up this hole for me, please ma’m. I tore it gettin’ th’ough the fence.”

“Le’s see. H-e-e h-e-e,” she laughed, “you sho it to’e it, Honey. Whyn’t chu go put on anudder wais’?”

“Uch-ur-o-o-h, Gran’ma git after me.”

“Fer t’arin’ yo’ wais’? Shucks! Ole Mis’ know chillun ’fo’ dis.”

“No’m. She git after me ’cause I come th’ough the wire fence, and she told me not to, and I forgot.”

Aunt Betsey looked at him sternly for a moment, then— “Ph-e-e,” and her face broke into a smile. “Well, Ah’ll ha’ t’ fix it fer you den. Chilluns does fergits.” Then she began a search for her needle—all the while talking to herself. “Now whar is dat needle done got to? Didn’ put ’tin my wais’,”— feeling for it—“Naw, ’tain’t dar. In my shawl? ’Tain’t dar. Ah wunner ef—Baby is you seed dat ole black, strange torm- cat, whut been hanging roun’ de yard, t’day?”

“Yes’m. Soon this mornin’.”

“Well,” she said, relieved, “maybe Um wrong—whar is dat needle done gone to?—but Ah been ’spicionin’ dat cat fer a witch ever sence he been comin’ roun’ hyere; en you got t’ be mighty kyereful ’ca’se ef hit’s a witch en hit gits hol’ uv any uv yo’ pins er needles, she li’ble t’ gi’ you a heap a trouble ’fo’ you kin stop it. Hah, *hyere hit!*” And she pulled the needle and a ball of homespun thread out of a crack in the wall. “Ah thought Ah ’membered put’n’ it ’way somewhar. Now come ’ere. Wait a minute—Ah lak t’ fergot,” and she went to the wood-box and got a piece of wood about the size of a pencil. “Put dis in yo’ mouf w’ile Ah sews you up, en keep it dar.”

“Whut witches do to you, Ai’ Betsey?” asked John.

“Lawd, Honey, dey do’s a plenty. Dey rides you at night twel you cain’ sleep. Dey tangles yo’ ha’r up so you cain’ hardly cyard it. Dey makes de fresh milk sour on you er de cow kick you. Now, ef you fin' a pin wid de p'int twoge you, dat's a sign uv good luck, haid t' you—bad luck. You mus' make a cross mark den, 'fo' you pick it up. En ef you fin's one in de path, don' kyere whichaway de haid is, you got t' make a cross mark en spit in it 'fo' you picks it up, 'ca'se a witch mout a lef' it dar t' ketch you. But ef you do dat, whutever meanness she 'uz gwi do t' you will go back on her. You allus mus' 'member dat."

"Whut do witches look like, Ai' Betsey—folks?"

"Look jes lak anything dey wan' to, Honey, folkses some-times, er cows, er dawgs, er chickens, er anything. But mos'ly, dey be's lak cats—ole black tormcats. You got t' watch dem."

"Did you ever see a witch, Ai' Betsey," John asked—eyes wide open.

"L-a-wd, Honey, h-h-m-m, m-any's de—," she paused to look up impressively; then—"*Keep* dat stick in *yo' mouf,* Honey. You kin talk wid it dar."

"Yes'm," and John put it back.

"Now whut wuz it chu ast me?"

"'At witch, Ai' Betsey. D'ju see him good? Whut he look like?"

"Yes, Honey, Ah's seed 'em—many's de times. Hit w-u-z— lemme s-e-e—hit wuz de yeah you wuz bawn, dat's when hit wuz, en you didn' do nothin' but cry en make a racket. You allus could make a heap a fuss, tee-hee!" From the laugh and the smile that went with it, John gathered that she approved his noisiness. "Dey wuz afeard you wa'n't gwi live, you wuz sorta puny-lak en mighty colicky," she went on, "but Ah knowed better'n dat, 'ca'se jes ez soon's Ah hyeahd you wuz bawn Ah sot out a ellum saplin' in de cornder uv my gyarden en name hit fer you, en hit growed right off, en hit's growin' yit. Dat's one sign whut don' nevuh fail, en—jes look how fat you is now."

John smiled appreciatively, but he wanted witches. "Whut 'at ole witch do, Ai' Betsey," he asked.

"Baby, ef you don't keep dat stick in yo' mouf w'ile Um sewin' yo' clo's up on you, Um gwi quit sewin' *en talkin'*, too. Hit's de wust kin' uv luck ef you don' do dat." The stick went back—this time to stay.

"Well, ez Ah said, dis hap'm in de fall uv de yeah you wuz bawn in. Now, Honey, dar's a heap a things you's got t' l'arn, en dat's howcome Um's tellin' you. Some folks sez a witch rides a broom en hit may be dey does. Ah don' know 'bout dat, but Ah does know dey'll ride you en you kin keep 'em out'n de house wid a broom, er salt en pepper, er sometimes sulphur. But de broom's de bes', en a saige-grass broom wid no handle in it is de bes' uv all. You 'member dat, now. Well, one e'nin', lak Ah said, Ah lent my broom t' my Sis Sallie 'ca'se her'n got burnt up w'en she set it too close t' de fiah-place en hit fell in de fiah w'en she went t' de woodpile fer a turn uv wood. En she fergot t' fetch mines back lak she said she would. Dar wuz a stray black cat wid yaller eyes, whut been hanging' roun' her house en mine all day, en Ah allus did b'lieve dat wuz de ole cat-witch en he knock Sis Sallie's broom in de fiah on puppose so he could git 'er; en w'en she got mine he knowed hit warn't no use; so den he come atter me." Aunt Betsey was through sewing by now and was scarcely conscious of John's presence. He had drawn a little stool to her feet and leaned against her, elbows on her knees and eyes fastened on her face. She looked away off into the distance, but didn't see the trees nor the skies with the clouds hanging in them. Memory was gathering its threads. "Well," she went on, "hit wuz late bedtime, hit wuz, de fiah wuz mighty nigh out, en Ah wuz jes thinkin' 'bout gwine t' sleep w'en dat ole witch hollered lak a cat. Ah knowed hit warn't no cat, dough, en Ah got up t' look fer de broom t' lay cross de do' 'fo' Ah 'membered Sis Sallie had it. Den Ah stop up de keyhole, Ah did, so she couldn' git in dar, en sprinkle salt en pepper all over de flo', so ef she did git in somehow, her feets 'ud git burnt. Ah laid down den en went t' sleep. Ah knowed Ah wuz safe. Atter Ah got t' sleep, Ah hyeahd a scufflin' gwine on, on de flo', en sump'm say, 'Oh my feets, dey's burnin' up! Oh my feets, dey's burnin' up!' Den Ah knowed she done got in some way er 'nudder, en de salt en pepper done cotch her. Ah grab de salt-cup f'um whar Ah put it behime m' piller en op'm de do' fer t' look fer her skin t' put salt in it so she cain' nevuh go back to it. But jes ez soon ez Ah op'm de do', she run out, she did, en grab dat skin off'n de groun' en lit over de palin's, she did, jes lak a whole passel uv dawgs 'uz atter her.

"Nex' mo'nin', Ah foun' out how she got in. She tuck a long brass pin en push dat stuffin' out de keyhole whar Ah put it en come in dat way. Dat ole witch ain' bothered me no mo' atter dat, not me, she ain't."

"But, Ai' Betsey," asked John, "how she come th'ough a keyhole? A keyhole's *little*."

"Ah knows hit is, Baby, but dat's de onliest way she kin come in ef de do's locked en de winder's shet. Hit's dissaway, chile. Ef de do's op'm, dey ha' t' come in jes lak folkses come in, 'ca'se dey is folkses w'en all's said en done. So ef de do's op'm en de winder ain't shet, dey comes in jes lak folkses would. But ef de do's shet en de winder's shet too, den de onliest way whut she kin git in a-tall is th'ough de keyhole in de do', 'ca'se dey ain' no keyhole in de winder. But 'fo' she kin do dat, she ha' t' shed her skin en leave it whar she kin git it w'en she come out. Den she kin make herself li'l en come th'ough any kin' uv keyhole, she kin."

"Cain' she come th'ough the cat-hole, Ai' Betsey?" asked John, wonderingly.

"Whut's d-a-t?" She looked at the little fellow intently, startled, even awed. "My G-a-w-d! How come it all dese yeahs Ah nevuh thought uv dat? Hit's jes lak Ole Mis' read out'n de Bible—'Out'n de mouvs uv babes en sucklin's comes wisdom.' Baby, Ah sho b'lieves you got de insight, en atter dis, dat ole cat uv mine sho got t' do her rat-ketchin' in de day-time, 'ca'se Um gwi fix dat cat-hole dis e'nin', sho!"

GRIEVIN'

B-a-b-y!" Aunt Betsey was calling John. "U-r-r-h Baby!"

John answered from away out in the pea-patch back of the cow lot, where he and John the Baptist were catching grass-hoppers, "M-a-a-'m?"

"Ef you don' come on hyere t' me, boy, dey ain' no tellin' whut Um gwi do t' you." Her words promised anything—tortures even, but her voice carried that never failing note of tenderness that was always in it when she spoke to John. He came running, for in Aunt Betsey's voice John heard another promise—she had something for him.

Aunt Nervy was sitting by the fireplace when John, all out of breath, rushed up. "Here me, Ai' Betsey, whutchu got me?" he asked and then said quickly, "Good e'nin'—good mo'nin', Ai' Nervy, is you well?" He had saved his manners before Aunt Betsey could remind him. Now he turned to her again and his eyes were dancing—expecting something. "Whutchu got f'me?" he asked eagerly.

But Aunt Betsey was looking at him sternly, "Howcome you ain' answer me w'en Ah fus' call you?" she demanded.

"I *did*, I *did*, Ai' Betsey. I answered you jus' soon's you call me, an' I run all de way an' I fell down an' skin' my han', too." The indignant John held out the proof, "See dar?"

But the old woman was not yet through with her examina-tion. "Whar wuz you at when Ah call you?" she asked him next.

"Me an' John de Baptis' wuz in de pea-patch catchin' hop-pergrasses," he answered.

"Oh, you wuz, wuz you? En ain't Ah hyearn Ole Mis' tell you *not* t' go in dat pea-patch not 'ntwel de djew wuz off'n de grass? Ain't Ah hyearn her tell you dat?" she demanded accusingly.

John hung his head and answered, "No'm."

"*Baby!*" There was surprise in her voice and pain too. "You look at me right good, Honey," she said gently, "didn' Ole Mis' tell you dat?"

"Dat wuz yistiddy, Ai' Betsey," said John virtuously. "She ain' tole me nothin' t'day."

"O-o-h, she ain't? Den whut she say when you ast 'er?"

"She didn' say nothin', Ai' Betsey," explained John. "You see when I went upstairs to ask her, she wuz readin' the Bible an' I didn' want to 'sturb her, so me an' John de Baptis' jus' went on out dar 'ca'se he wuz hungry."

"Sis Nervy," Aunt Betsey said smilingly, "You jes cain' head chillun off, dese days en times, kin you? Nobody but Gawd hisse'f knows whut de worl' is comin' to." Then to John she said, "Come 'ere, Honey, en le' me feel you en see ef you's wet."

He stood close to her while she felt his trousers and waist. "You ain' wet none t' h'ut," she said to him. "You kin run 'long, now, Um th'ough wid you."

"Naw, you ain't, Ai' Betsey," said John, swinging on her arm and looking into her twinkling eyes. "Whutchu got fer me?"

"Ah ain' got nothin' fer you!"

"Yes, you *is*, Ai' Betsey, you *know* you is," insisted John.

When Aunt Betsey denied it again, Aunt Nervy spoke up, "Quit teasin' dat boy, Sis Betsey. She ain' got nothin' fer you, Honey," she said to John, "but yo' Ai' Nervy's got a kitten fer you up t' her house en us is gwine up dar en git it right now."

Aunt Betsey went along with them, or rather with Aunt Nervy, for John ran on ahead and got there long before they did.

He found the kittens, four of them, in a box behind Aunt Nervy's door, and he immediately fell in love with all of them. He wanted them all, but two had already been promised, and of those left, one was a puny, sickly little fellow that couldn't live long anyway. Aunt Nervy said that if it didn't die itself right soon, she was going to have it killed.

"Whut you goin' kill it fer?" demanded John.

"Ca'se hit's sickly en no'count, Honey," she answered.

John was puzzled. "You kill 'im 'cause he sick?" he asked.

Then Aunt Nervy explained that when anything was sick like that it never would be of any account and you had to kill it because it would be in the way.

John's sympathy went out to the little sickly kitten. For his own he had picked the biggest in the box, but he couldn't bear to think of that kitten's being killed. "Do you kill eve'ything 'at gits sick like dat?" he asked, and when Aunt Nervy said, "Yes, eve'ything," he wanted to know if she meant babies too.

"My Gawd, Baby, naw!" she exclaimed, "dey's chilluns!"

"A kitten's a cat's chillun, ain't it?" John asked.

The two old women laughed at this, and soon Aunt Betsey told him to get his kitten and come on home with her. John was torn between two desires. He wanted the biggest kitten, but he didn't want the little kitten killed. After a silent struggle the sickly kitten won. He picked it up and started to the door.

"Baby," said Aunt Betsey almost pleadingly, "you don' want dat'n. Git one uv de udders."

But John's mind was made up—he wanted that one. "You see, Ai' Betsey," he explained, holding the tiny little kitten tightly against his breast with both hands, "hit's dissaway. Dis li'l kitten may be sick a long, long time befo' hit gits well, en I got t' feed it an' nuss it so hit won't die." These simple childish words from trembling lips found sympathetic ears, but it was the tenderness that looked out from the little fellow's eyes that touched their hearts more than tears ever could have done. The two old women looked at each other.

"Whutchu think uv dat, Sis Betsey?" Aunt Nervy asked.

"Ah ain't thinkin', Sis Nervy," Aunt Betsey answered softly, "Um jes thankin' Gawd fer it right dis minute. A-man!"

And Aunt Nervy echoed, "A-man!"

Aunt Betsey named the kitten "Cephus," and it began to improve at once but was never very playful. It would rather lie in John's lap and sleep. He wanted to take it to bed with him but Grandma said "No sir! Fleas will eat you up." Aunt Betsey added that the cat might suck his breath and kill him.

After a while the kitten began to get weaker and John nursed harder than ever. When the little boy put it down, the kitten would cry until he took it up again.

One morning John found the kitten lying under his chair in the yard—it was cold and stiff. He ran to the kitchen, "Ai' Betsey," he begged, "come see whut's de matter wi' Cephus, please ma'm. He won't move."

"In a minute, Honey," she answered. "Did you call 'im?"

"Yessum, I called 'im an' called 'im an' called 'im, an he won't move. An' I put my han' on him," his frightened voice went on, "an' he's right cold an' stiff."

"Ah spec' dat little kitten's daid, Honey," she said kindly.

"Naw he ain't dead, Ai' Betsey"; John's lips were trembling. "He ain't dead 'cause I been nussin' 'im good. Come on, Ai' Betsey," and he caught her apron and pulled her to the door.

She took his hand in hers and went with him to the kitten. "Yeah, Honey, hit's daid," she said after a bit, and then she added gently, "Ah spec' hit wuz lookin' fer you when hit died."

John pressed his face against Aunt Betsey and the tears he had been fighting back came in torrents. "Don'chu cry lak dat, Baby," she tried to say cheerfully, "Us gwi gitchu anudder kitten right off."

"I don't want no udder kitten, Ai' Betsey," the little voice wailed, "I want my Cephus cat," and then he ran to hide his grief in the corner of the kitchen chimney. Aunt Betsey followed and tried to comfort him. When his tears continued to come, she got a chair and seated herself near him. "Hiesh, Baby, hiesh!" she begged. "Don'chu cry no mo 'lak dat, hiesh! Dat li'l kitten's a heap better off, he is; he ain' suff'rin' none a-tall now."

"Oh, Ai' Betsey," the smothered voice sobbed from between his hands, "he wuz such a little feller—he wuz such a little feller."

"Baby, you come 'ere t' me. Come t' yo' ole black mammy whut's nuss you all yo' life. Come on, Honey." John came to her and buried his face in her lap—his little body shaken with sobs. Aunt Betsey pressed his head with her hands. "Hiesh, Baby," she begged again, and then, as a sob rose in her own throat, she said, "Lawd, Ah knows how he feels. Lawd, *you know* Ah knows," and then to John, "Hiesh, Baby, hiesh! Come on up in yo' ole mammy's lap, Um gwi tell you sump'm."

She held John to her tightly for a long, long minute, and then she said, "Um gwi tell you 'bout my baby boy, Sammy." After another pause she went on, "Now dis wuz back in ole Ferginny, Baby, way 'fo' de wah, hit wuz, en 'fo' me en Ole Mis' en Ole Marster, whut wuz yo' grandaddy, en all de res' uv de folkses come t' Mis'sippi t' live. Ah done had two chillun when dat boy wuz bawn—bofe gals, dey wuz, Sallie wuz de oldes' en den Tabby. En when he come a boy, Ah sho wuz glad, en proud too. Ole Mis' en Ole Marster wuz glad ez Ah wuz en Ole Mis' made 'im some p'utty clo's, en when Ah ax her whut us gwi name 'im, she say, 'Sam-u-el.' So us name 'im dat, us did, but us call 'im 'Sammy' fer sho't.

"De moon wa'n't right when he wuz bawn; hit 'uz wanin' en losin' strengt' hard. Dat's a bad time fer birthin' chillun, hit is, Honey, 'ca'se dey loses strengt' wid de moon. But dat didn' worrit me none den, 'ca'se Ah wuz young en didn' know nothin' t' whut Ah knows now. Sammy allus wuz puny en sickly-lak en Ole Mis' le' me keep him up at de kitchen wid me all day long. Us raise 'im t' be fo' yeahs ole come a mont', us did, en when Ole Mis' come out in de yard he foller her roun' jes lak a dawg; en eve'y li'l w'ile, w'ile he foll'in 'er he'd say, 'Ole Mis',' en when she say, 'Whutchu want, Sammy?' he jes clap his han's, he would, en laugh en say, 'Nothin',' en den dey bofe 'ud laugh. He sho did love Ole Mis', dat boy did; all us done dat, but Ah b'lieve dat baby love her de mos'es uv all.

"Well, one Sa'day one us neighbors, Mist' Huff, hit wuz, whut live 'bout twelve miles off 'cross de creek, gi'n his niggers a barbecue, en dat Sa'day he sont Ole Marster word t' let his niggers come. Ole Marster le'm go, he did, mos' nigh all uv'm. Jes atter us fo'd de creek, Big Creek dey call it, whut wuz mos' t' Mars Jim's—dat 'uz Mars Jim Huff, hit wuz, whar us 'uz gwine—a owul holler out in de woods. Dat's a bad sign, spesh'ly in de daytime, but us 'uz feelin' good, us wuz, en us sung out t'gedder, 'You kin holler, Mist' Owul but you cain' foller me!' En den us lock us li'l fingers, us did, en pull hard t' choke 'im. Ah don' b'lieve, dough, us pull hard 'nough. Hit 'gun t' cloud up right atter us got dar en look lak hit gwine come a rain, but us didn' kyere 'bout dat, 'ca'se de barbecue wuz in de 'bac'er barn en us knowed us 'uz all right.

"Atter us done et en whilest de folkses wuz cleanin' off de tables en movin' 'em so's dey could dance, me bein' a house nigger all my life, Ah knowed my manners, Ah did, en Ah went up t' de big house t' see Mars Jim en Miss Millie en pass de time a day en see how dey wuz so's Ah could tell Ole Mis'. Whilest Ah wuz up dar wid 'em, hit started t' rain. My Lawd, Baby, how hit did come down! En hit jes kep' a-comin'. You couldn' see 'cross de yard, much less see de barn out by de corn-crib.

"Atter w'ile, hit 'uz mos' fo' 'clock den, en de rain wuz still comin' down, Mars Jim said he reggin us 'ud ha' t' stay all night dar, 'ca'se atter a rain lak dat d' wa'n't no crossin' de fo'd 'fo' nex' day, nohow. Us didn' kyere 'bout dat, dough, 'ca'se us know us 'ud ha' a good time. Well suh, Ah jes done started t' run back t' de barn, whedder er no, when sump'm hit me in my chis' f'um de inside, en den dat sump'm started pullin' me twoge home. Ah knowed whut 'twuz right off, en Ah say 'Mars Jim, Ah got t' go home—my baby's tuck sick,' en when he ax me how Ah know, Ah tell 'im Ah kin feel it. He say den, he did, dat dey wa'n't no way fer nobody t' cross dat creek now 'fo' de nex' e'nin', 'ca'se hit up all over de bottoms right den. Hit wuz, too; 'ca'se you could see it f'um de house.

"Ah tried t' res' my min', en Ah went out t' de 'bac'er barn whar de folkses wuz dancin', but hit wa'n't no use; Ah jes kep' feelin' dat baby callin' me, en Ah knowed hit wuz bad sick. 'Long 'bout sundown Ah jes couldn' stan' hit no longer en Ah tole Mars Jim dat Ah wuz jes 'bleeged t' git 'cross somehow, en w'en he see how worrit Ah wuz he say dat maybe ef Ah went roun' by Benton Ah could cross de bridge whut 'uz by de railroad track whar de creek went under it. Benton wuz ten miles f'um Mars Jim's en ten miles f'um home, en de

"De bridge wuz gone—done wash' away"

creek wuz fo' miles f'um Benton twoge home. Ah wuz gwi walk it, but Mars Jim lont me a mule t' ride, en he gi'n one us boys a mule t' go wid me, en he sont one uv his own niggers 'long t' fetch de mules back. De rain done hilt up when us started but soon hit put in t' drizzlin' right stiddy. Ah had on a heavy close-weave coat whut Miss Millie's cook lont me; so Ah didn't git wet cep'm my feets, but hit wa'n't no time 'fo' de boys wuz wet plum th'ough.

"Ah nevuh is seed ez much watter in all my life, Honey," she said as John nestled closer, "hit wuz eve'ywhar—de roads wuz kivered, en de fiel's wuz kivered en de ditches wuz full. En 'way off to one side us, us could hyeah dat creek ro'rin'. De moon wuz up, but de clouds wuz so thick hit didn' do much good, en when us got t' de bridge a li'l atter midnight, de bridge wuz gone—done wash' away! Ah mos' died, Ah did, 'ca'se hit look lak Ah wuz stop fer sho dis time, en all night long—mighty nigh eve'y step us took, Ah could feel my Sammy callin' me. De boys wan' t' go back but Ah said Ah wuz gwi cross on de trussle en walk—hit wa'n't but six miles. So Mars Jim's boy tu'n back wid de mules en us cross on de trussle en put out.

"When us got home, hit wuz mos' day, hit wuz, en Ah seed a light shinin' in my house en when Ah got t' de do' Ah hyeah my baby say right weak-lak, 'Mammy—Mammy—Mammy,' jes lak dat. Ole Mis' 'uz dar jes lak she allus wuz when de folks be sick. When Ah come in, she had de baby in her lap en she ain' say nothin', but her eyes ax me whar Ah been all dat time. Den Ah tell her de creek riz, en Ah ax 'er ef he sick much. Ole Mis' jes han' 'im to me en say he been callin' me all night. Gawd! How hot he wuz! En he jes tu'n dis way en dat. Terreckly he say ag'in, 'Mammy—Mammy,' but his eyes wuz shet. En w'en he done dat, Ah lif' him up high en hilt him close t' me en Ah say, 'Op'm yo' eyes, Baby, en look. Hyere's yo' mammy done come t' you, Honey.' He op'm 'em den, he did, en sorta half smile at fus', en den he put his li'l han' 'g'inst my face en push it off. He push hit off, he did, en he say, 'Go 'way, Ah wants my Mammy.' He didn' know me, Honey, he *didn'* know me." Aunt Betsey swallowed back a sob and pulled John up to her—tight. "En den," she went on, "he died. Ah jes set dar en hilt 'im, Ah did, 'ntwel 'way atter sunrise, en Ah couldn' cry ner nothin', but Ah jes hilt 'im en ache.

"Gawd gi's you tears t' wash yo' sor'rs away, Honey, but mines didn' come twel jes 'fo' my nex' baby wuz bawn; en right now, in de night-time when de rain is fallin' Ah kin hyeah dat baby callin' me—'Mammy—Mammy—Mammy.'

"Dar's a heap a sor'rs in dis worl', Baby, en dar is few dat tears won' wash away; en Ah spec' dat one uv dem kin'— de maines' one uv 'em—is losin' a baby lak dat.

"So, you see, Baby, Ah knows how you is feelin' right now; en Ah knows you knows Ah knows how you feels; en Ah knows you gwi listen t' yo' ole mammy when she tell you not t' cry no mo' 'bout dat kitten; en Um gwi make Net wash dem dishes, en us—jes me en you—is gwine out in de pea-patch en pick de peas fer dinner; en whilest us is pickin' 'em, Um gwi tell you a tale 'bout Brer Rabbit."

BRER MOLE SWAPS HIS EYES FER BRER
FRAWG'S TAIL

Man, suh, see dat frawg yon'er? Ketch 'im en le's see ef us kin fin' whar his tail wuz at," said Uncle Alford one morning. Aunt Betsey warned from the kitchen window, "Kyereful—kyereful now, Baby. 'Member whut Ah tole you 'bout warts." Holding the frog carefully by the hind legs so that there wasn't any chance of getting warts from him, John and Uncle Alford looked hard and long for "whar de tail nuse t' be at."

"Well," said the old man, "by rights, hit ought t' be right hyere, but hit's been so long sence he had aire'n, Ah reggin de place done growed plum off."

"Whut 'come of his tail, Unc' Alfo'd?" asked John, noticing for the first time that a frog didn't have a tail as everything else did. "Did he lose it?"

"Ah dunno. You see hit's been sich a long time ago sence hit hap'm dat Ah disremembers jes zac'ly how hit come 'bout. Ah spec' ef you ax Sis Betsey," he went on, "she could tell you 'bout it."

But Aunt Betsey was interested herself. "Gwon en tell 'im

'bout it, Brer Alfo'd. Don'chu see he jes eechin' fer it? Gwon en tell 'bout it, nigger," she went on, "dat is—dat is, ef you spec's t' eat *hyere* dis mo'nin'. 'Sides dat, Ah ain' hyeahd 'bout it in a long time, m'se'f."

Uncle Alford gave up. "Well, Ah reggin Ah is got time fer it 'twixt now en breakfus' en hitchin' up dem mules. Ah wunner," he broke in musingly and with a decided touch of resentment, "Ah wunner howcome Mars John say hitch up mules dis mo'nin'? Dem hosses ain' tiah'd. Harnesses jes nach'ly don' fit on a mule, dey don't, no mo' 'n a jimswinger coat fits on a nigger. Dress 'em bofe up dattaway, en dey bofe uv 'em wush you hadn' done it."

"Ah don' b'lieves you laks eggs fer breakfus' wid yo' ham en gravy, does you, Brer Alfo'd?" Aunt Betsey asked significantly. "Dey's a little skase roun' yere right now."

"Yes *ma'm*, Sis Betsey. You *knows* Ah does dat!"

"Well, den," she said a little more significantly; so Uncle Alford began.

"Well suh, in dem days Brer Frawg had a tail en no eyes, whilest Brer Mole, whut live in de groun', had eyes en no tail. One day w'en Brer Frawg wuz passin' 'long de road, he come by Brer Mole's house, en Brer Mole, whut 'uz sunnin' hisse'f by de do', 'vited 'im t' come in en set en chaw aw'ile en spread de news. So he sot down, he did, en bofe uv 'em tuck a big chaw uv 'bac'er, en atter Brer Frawg ax 'im 'bout how Sis Mole en de two chillun wuz gittin' along, he say, 'Howcome hit wuz dat you wuzn't out t' de church las' Sunday t' hyeah de Elder preach? Wuz you sick?'

" 'Well—not t' say jes zac'ly sick, Brer Frawg,' sez Brer Mole, sezzee, 'but Ah did had a little tech uv rheumatiz in m' j'ints, en 'sides dat, Ah don' lak t' go t' chu'ch ner nowhar ilse in de daytime, 'ca'se de light hu'ts m' eyes. En twixt dat en de mis'ry in m' j'ints, Ah thought Ah'd jes stay at home. Whut he preach 'bout, Brer Frawg?'

" "'Bout de sins uv de worl' en de temptations uv de devul. En *man,* he *preached!*—he sho did preach! Brer Jaybird hisse'f 'uz mightily teched, he wuz, en quit qua'elin' fer a w'ile, he did, en ole Jedge Owul 'low dat ef dey could git de Elder t' cah'y on de stracted meetin' dat start nex' mont', maybe he could 'suade Brer Jaybird into de chu'ch en 'way f'um 'is weekit ways.'

"Dey talk on lak dat fer a wi'le, dey did, en atterw'ile Brer Frawg he 'low, 'Ah been thinkin', Brer Mole, dat ef havin' eyes gwi keep you 'way f'um meetin's en sich, you'd be better off ef you git shet uv dem eyes.' But Brer Mole say dem eyes 'uz a heap a he'p to 'im at times. Den Brer Frawg he 'low, 'Dat is so, butchu know de Bible says hit's a heap mo' better t' be saved blin' dan hit wuz t' be los' seein'. You know dat.'

"Dey arg'ed wid one anudder conside'ble, dey did, en twoge de las' Brer Mole say, 'How in de name uv Gawd you spec' me t' git along wid no eyes ner nothin'?' Den Brer Frawg say, 'Gitchu a tail jes lak whut mine is. Dey is de bes', en den you kin git along widout no trouble a-tall.'

"Dey arg'ed some mo', dey did, en den Brer Mole ax 'im whar he gwi git a tail lak his'n, en Brer Frawg say dat seein' ez him en Brer Mole 'uz mighty good frien's, en 'sides all dat, seein' dat dem eyes 'uz keepin' Brer Mole 'way f'um de chu'ch, he b'lieved dat de Lawd done put it on 'im t' he'p Brer Mole. So dat bein' ez 'twuz, he 'uz willin', ef Brer Mole wuz, t' swap his tail fer dem eyes whut 'uz troub'lin' Brer Mole so. But Brer Mole 'uz a mighty close trader, he wuz, en he 'low dat fer t' swap a good pa'r uv eyes fer a secon'han' tail wa'n't no fair swap en he wouldn' do it, he wouldn'.

"En den Brer Frawg riz up, he did, en say his tail wa'n't no mo' secon'han' 'n whut Brer Mole's eyes wuz; but Brer Mole p'int out, he did, dat Brer Frawg say hisse'f dat he nuse de tail all de time, en dat he know *he* don' nuse his eyes cep'm once in a w'ile w'en he go t' chu'ch er some sich a matter. So dem eyes uv his'n 'uz jes nach'ly boun' t' be de newes' en de bestes' uv de two. Brer Frawg knowed he had 'im dar; so he ax 'im how much boot he want, en Brer Mole say he want fo' bits. Brer Frawg won' hyeah t' dat, dough, 'ca'se he say he know whar he kin buy a bran' new pa'r fer six bits en keep 'is tail, too.

"Well, dey arg'ed some mo', but dey couldn' come t' no 'greement. So Brer Frawg say, 'Well, good day, Brer Mole,' en started off lak he gwi leave. 'Fo' he got t' de gate, Brer Mole call 'im back en say dat seein' ez how dey 'uz allus sich gre't frien's en dat he didn' want Brer Frawg t' think he 'uz tryin' t' 'vantage 'im, he b'lieved dat ef Brer Frawg 'ud th'ow in a plug uv 'bac'er he'd make de swap. Brer Frawg he 'greed t' dat, he did, en dey done it.

"Brer Frawg en Brer Mole sorta fight shy uv one anudder ever sence den, 'ca'se bofe uv'm 'uz skeered de udder'n 'uz gwi wan' t' rue back, en dey bofe wuz satterfied jes ez dey wuz."

WHY ELEFUNTS IS SKEERED UV MICES

Big man," said Uncle Alford one morning, "is you gwine t' de succus w'en hit come nex' week?" It was Sunday and Uncle Alford was busy shining Mars John's shoes, making ready for church; and, as usual, John was watching him.

"Yes suh," he answered, "an' you is too, Unc' Alfo'd; 'cause Uncle John said you had to go to drive us. Ain't you glad?"

"Well, dat's better, Ah spec'. Ah wuz gwi git you t' ax dat man sump'm, but Ah spec' Ah better ax 'im m'se'f."

"Whut man you talking 'bout?" asked the boy.

"Dat man whut owns de succus. Ah wan' t' ax 'im ef de elefunts is still skeered uv mices lak dey nuseter be."

"Skeered of mices?" laughed John derisively, "You know a mice can't hurt no elephant, Unc' Alfo'd, 'cause he's big as a house."

"Cain' hu't 'im?" the shoe brush was still for a wondering second. "Lawd, m-a-n, whut is you talkin' about? Ain't Ah nevuh tole you 'bout dat? Ah ain't? Well suh, you jes listen t' me. Brer Elefunt been doing jes 'bout lak he please fer de longes', 'ca'se he so big. He jes run over eve'ybody, he did, en done 'em jes lak he wan' to, dat is, twel he run up ag'ins' Brer Rabbit. *He* fix 'im. He sho did fix 'im, 'ca'se ef Brer Rabbit ain' big, he got a heap a sense, he is.

"Now dis is de way hit hap'm. One day Brer Elefunt 'uz feelin' sorta hongry-lak en devilish, en he mash down Brer Rabbit's fence en 'stroyed 'is pea-patch—didn' lef' 'im nothin'. Dem whut he ain't et, he tromp down. En Brer Rabbit come up, he did, en Man, suh, he 'uz mad! He rah'd, he did, en he pitch en he cuss Brer Elefunt sump'm scan'lous. De folkses come up dey did en listen, en Brer Elefunt 'gun t' git mad hisse'f en 'vited Brer Rabbit t' fight en see ef he could fight ez big ez he could cuss. Brer Rabbit didn' wan' to do dat, dough, en Brer Elefunt laugh en say he 'uz skeered. Brer Rabbit 'low, he did, dat he wa'n't skeered uv 'im ner nobody ilse, but ef he th'ow Brer Elefunt lak he know he could, he 'uz too light t' hol' 'im, en dat wa'n't fair. Den Brer Elefunt say ef Brer Rabbit cain' hol' 'im, fer him t' stan' up en knock it out like a man ought to, en jes t' show 'im he 'uz a man hisse'f, he'd shet bofe his eyes tight en gi' Brer Rabbit de fus' two licks. Eve'ybody say dat 'uz fair enough. So Brer Rabbit 'greed t' dat en say he fight 'im de nex' day. Den he went home walkin' a heap sassier den whut he felt.

"Well, Brer Rabbit 'uz worrit a lot, he wuz, 'ca'se he knowed he didn' ha' no chance ef he fit Brer Elefunt man t' man. He ain' tole Sis Rabbit yit 'bout whut 'uz comin' off de nex' day, en he 'uz settin' by de fiah stud'in' 'bout whut he gwi ha' t' do en waitin' fer his supper, w'en Sis Rabbit gi'n a screech, she did, en jump up on de kitchen table. En w'en he ax her whut 'uz de matter, she said fer him t' kill dat mice 'ca'se he tried t' run up her laig. En w'en he laugh, she started t' th'ow de rollin'-pin at 'im, en de fryin' pan, too, twel he tole her whut he 'uz thinkin' 'bout. So, dat night dey sot de rat-trap in de crib, en de nex' mo'nin' hit 'uz full uv mices. He cram his pockets full uv 'em, he did, en went to whar de fight 'uz gwi be at.

"Eve'ybody 'uz dar en Brer Elefunt too, en he 'uz lookin' mighty vi-grous, he wuz. De folkses made a ring, en jes 'fo' Brer Rabbit en Brer Elefunt step in it, Brer Rabbit say out loud so eve'ybody could hyeah 'im, 'W'en Ah gits th'ough wid dis little job, Brer Fox, sposen you en me go fishin'.' En Brer Fox laugh, he did, en didn' say nothin'. Brer Elefunt 'spicioned sump'm 'uz up, en didn' wan' t' shet his eyes, but ole Jedge Owul 'uz dar en he said a 'greement wuz a 'greement en fair wuz fair, en Brer Elefunt had 'greed t' shet bofe his eyes en gi' Brer Rabbit de fus' two licks, en ef he didn' do it, he 'uz gwi fine 'im a bar'l uv scaly-barks en maybe put 'im in de callyboose, too. Den Brer Rabbit say he didn' aim t' break de skin on Brer Elefunt; he 'uz jes gwi tap 'im two light licks on de end uv his snout en atter dat Brer Elefunt could do whut he wan' to. So Brer Elefunt shet his eyes, he did, en stuck out his snout, en den Brer Rabbit step up to 'im en push one uv dem mices up Brer Elefunt's snout. 'One lick,' sezzee, en he push de udder un up wid de udder han'. 'Two licks,' sezzee, en he step back out'n de way. L-a-w-d, he'd better! Dem mices thought dey'd foun' a new hole en went up it, en Brer Ele-funt thought de devul had 'im! Dem eyes come op'm, dey did, en dey got big ez soup plates! He twis' en he squirm en he holler, en eve'y once in a while Brer Rabbit step in quick-lak en hit 'im wid his fis'—kerplunk! En he tell 'im, 'Stan' up en fight lak a man!'

"Brer Elefunt gi'n a powerful snort"

"But Brer Elefunt didn' pay 'im no min'—he 'uz tryin' t' git shet uv dem devuls in 'is snout. Aw M-a-n-suh, you *jes ought t' seed 'im!* He rah'h, he did, en he romped. He stood on his hind foots en he stood on his front foots en he roll over en he stood on his haid, en he twis' en he turn en he wiggle. Den he tuck t' runnin' roun', he did, en he run over a tree big ez dat un by de woodpile en knock it flat. All de folkses got out'n de way, dey did, cep'm' Brer Addersnake, en Brer Elefunt step on 'is haid en nake en mash hit out so flat he spread all over de groun', en ever sence den, eve'ybody been call 'im 'Spreadin' Adder.'

"Well, atter w'ile Brer Elefunt gi'n a powerful snort, he did, en blowed dem two mices out on de groun', en w'en he see whut 'twuz he sho wuz mad—he mak lak he gwi start fer Brer Rabbit ag'in. W'en de done dat, Brer Rabbit pull two mo' mices out'n 'is pockits en started fer him. Brer Elefunt couldn' stan' dat, he couldn', so he jes flop dem yeahs uv his'n whut's big ez a quilt, en lef' dar.

"Ever sence den ef anybody jes shake a mice at 'im, he gone —he jes cain' stan' it.

"L-a-w-d, how dem folkses laugh! Brer Fox swo' he ain' nevuh see no succus whut 'uz ekil to it, en 'sides dat, he done won a bushel uv scaly-barks off'n his cousin, Brer Fox Squr'l, bettin' on dat fight, en he 'uz gwi 'vide 'em wid Brer Rabbit, en mo' 'n dat, fer de nex' two times dey go fishin', he 'uz gwi dig all de baits hisse'f.

"Naw, Honey, dey couldn' nevuh beat Brer Rabbit, dey couldn', 'ca'se dat's one somebody whut's sho got sense."

WHEN BRER RABBIT THUNDERED

One Sunday morning John was strutting around the hall with Uncle John's shoes on over his own and wishing that his feet were as big as Uncle John's. Presently Uncle Alford called, "Big Man, fetch me dem shoes 'fo' you w'ars 'em plum out; den d'won't be no nuse t' shine 'em."

The little fellow stalked up to him and said pleadingly, "They mos' fits, don't they, Unc' Alfo'd?"

The old man examined them critically. "Dey does now, fer a fac', suh! Me en Sis Betsey 'uz sayin', no longer 'n dis mo'nin', dat by one mo' Chris'mus, en sho'ly not mo'n two, you 'uz gwi be ez big er bigger 'n whut Mars John is right now. Takes dem shoes off, Honey, en ast Mars John t' gi' me a chaw uv 'bac'er. Ah needs de ambeer fer de blackin'." This was a regular Sunday routine—shine and "'bac'er" both.

When Uncle Alford asked for the tobacco, little John demurred—he wasn't quite ready to give up the shoes. "You already got some 'bac'er, Unc' Alfo'd."

"Ah knows Ah is, but de ambeer whut come f'um de 'bac'er Mars John nuses makes a heap de bes' ambeer fer shinin' shoes. Mine ain' no good fer dat. Run 'long now, en w'en you gits back Um got anudder tale Ah jes 'membered whut Ah got t' tell you."

"Whut it's about, Unc' Alfo'd? 'Bout Brer Rabbit an' the tar-baby?" he asked eagerly.

"Nunc, nunc! Hit's about Brer Rabbit aw right, en you better huh'y up 'fo' Ah fergits it."

When the "chaw" was properly settled in his mouth and the "ambeer" flowing freely, he continued, "Ah ain't nevuh tole you howcome hit is a rabbit is got a sho't tail en long yeahs, is Ah?"

John shook his head. "Naw suh," he answered.

"Well, dis is de way dat hap'm. Now uv co'se you 'members Ah done tole you dat in dem days animuls en birds en snakes en things en folkses, too, mixed about t'gedder a whole lot mo' 'n whut dey does now, en Ah reggin dat 'uz 'ca'se dey

could un'erstan' one anudder w'en dey talk, en eve'ybody
knowed jes zac'ly whut eve'ybody ilse 'uz sayin'.

"Now Brer Rabbit en Brer Fox 'uz gre't frien's, dey wuz,
en all de time fishin' en huntin' t'gedder. En one day dey wuz
huntin', en dey got tiah'd, en dey sot down, dey did, on a log
'side a de creek t' res'. Whilest dey 'uz restin' en talkin', a
big catfish come t' de top uv de water en look at 'em.

"Den Brer Fox he 'low—'Bless *Gawd*, Brer Rabbit, ef us
had us some hooks en lines us could ketch us a mess uv fish!'
En Brer Rabbit he love fish, he did, en he rummage roun' in
'is pockits en felt uv 'is clo's en at las' he say, 'Ah done foun'
a hook stickin' in my coat-tail whar Ah done hid it f'um m'
chillun.' (He 'uz w'arin' a jimswinger coat 'ca'se you know he
'uz allus a mighty stylish gent'mun, Brer Rabbit wuz.) 'But
Brer Fox,' he say, feelin' in all 'is pockits ag'in, 'Ah ain' got
narry piece uv line ner eb'm a straing. Is you?' Brer Fox he
look in 'is pockits ag'in, but he didn' ha' none en he 'low he
did, 'Now whut us gwi do?' Dey wuz mighty worrit by den,
en dey belly 'uz jes beggin' fer fish. Brer Rabbit 'lowed dey'd
ha' t' make 'm a line out'n sump'm, en den dey skint a young
hickory saplin' en tried t' make 'em a line out'n de bark, but it
'uz too big t' go in de hook-eye, en dar dey wuz.

"Well, w'en dey done mos' gi'n up, Brer Fox look at Brer
Rabbit's tail (hit 'uz longer den his'n wuz, en he didn' lak
dat), en he 'low, 'Ah tell you whut us do, Brer Rabbit, en us
kin ketch us a mess, *sho!* Le's tie dat hook on de end uv yo'
tail en you kin squat on de aige uv de bank en th'ow de hook
in. En w'en you gits a bite, ef hit's too big fer you t' pull out
yo'se'f, Ah'll be right yere to he'p you.' But Brer Rabbit 'uz
mighty proud uv his tail, he wuz, en he didn' wan' t' spile it.
So he say, 'Howcome us don' tie hit on yo' tail, Brer Fox?'
Den Brer Fox, he 'low his'n 'uz too sho't.

"Dey arg'ed, dey did, fer de longes'—fus' one en den de
udder, en atter w'ile Brer Rabbit bit off a chaw uv 'bac'er en

'low, he did, dat ez fur ez he 'uz consarned he wouldn' min'
it fer hisse'f, but 'is wife jes comb 'is tail fer 'im 'fo' he lef'
home, en ef he do dat he'd git hit all knotted up, en she'd be
mad wid 'im ef she had t' comb it ag'in. Dey arg'ed some mo',
dey did, en all de time dey wuz gittin' mo' en mo' fish-hongry.
Fus' en las', Brer Rabbit say he'd do it ef he could ha' de
bigges' fish. Brer Fox, he 'gree t' dat en say he dig de baits too.

"Well suh, Brer Rabbit he so fish-hongry by now twel he
fergit dat Brer Mud-Turkle whut live in de creek, had been
layin' fer him fer de longes' fer t' ketch 'im, eve'y sence he got
cotch in a daidfall whut Brer Rabbit sot in 'is watterme'm
patch en got mash' flat. He fergit dat, he did, en let Brer Fox
tie on de hook en bait it, en den he squat on de aige uv de
creek en th'owed de hook in. Brer Mud-Turkle he all de time
been listenin' t' whut dey wuz sayin', en ez soon ez Brer Rabbit's tail hit de watter, he grab it wid 'is mouf, right close up
t' de butt uv it, en gi'n a yank. Den Brer Rabbit he holler,
'Ah got 'im, Brer Fox! Ah got 'im, en he's a big 'un, too! He
done swollit hook, line, en all.'

"En all de time Brer Mud-Turkle 'uz tryin 't' pull 'im in
de creek en drown 'im. But Brer Rabbit dug his foots en han's
in de mud, he did, en hilt on.

"Brer Fox run up den, en w'en he see whut wuz de matter
he say, skeered-lak, 'L-a-w-d-y-mussey, Brer Rabbit, dat's Brer
Mud-Turkle whut's gotchu!'

"En Brer Rabbit say, 'Ur-r-r-h, My Gawd'lmighty, en he
won' tu'n lose twel hit thunder! Thunder, Brer Fox.'

"En Brer Fox, he laugh to hisse'f, he did, en say 'Ah dunno
how. You thunder yo'se'f, Brer Rabbit.'

"En Brer Rabbit he say, 'B-o-o-o-om! B-o-o-o-m! Boom-
boom!' En all de time he slippin' en he beggin' Brer Fox to
he'p 'im.

"Well, den, w'en he mos' in de creek, Brer Fox come down
to 'im en he say he couldn' reach nothin' cep'm 'is yeahs, en

Brer Rabbitt say fer him t' grab dem en *pull.* En he tuck hol' uv 'm, he did, en shet 'is eyes en *sot* back!

"Brer Rabbit's yeahs 'gun t' stretch, en Brer Fox 'low, sorta gruntin'-lak, 'You's comin', Brer Rabbit, jes hol' on. You's comin'!'

"But Brer Rabbit say, ''Tain't me, Brer Fox, hit's m' yeahs! *Pull,* Brer Fox, *pull!*"

"En w'en he see whut wuz, Brer Fox tuck anudder wrop roun' 'is han's wid dem yeahs en gi'n a powerful pull dis time, en Brer Rabbit's tail broke off right whar Brer Mud-Turkle 'uz hol'in' it, en out he come!

"En w'en Brer Rabbit cotch 'is bref, he see he didn' ha' no tail en' is yeahs 'uz long. Den he say t' Brer Fox, he did, 'Now look whut you done done!' En w'en Brer Fox laugh, he made a grab fer his gun en swo' he 'uz gwi kill 'im, but Brer Fox runned off, he did, en he hollered back—

> 'Brer Coon he got a ring-a-roun' tail,
> Brer Possum's ain' got no ha'r.
> Brer Fox got a p'utty, bushy tail,
> But Brer Rabbit ain' got none t' spar'.'

"Dey didn' speak t' one 'nudder atter dat fer de longes', dey didn', not twel ole Jedge Owul, whut wuz de jedge uv de co't en de moderater in de chu'ch, too, tol' 'em he 'uz gwi chu'ch 'em ef dey didn' 'have deyse'fs. Dey made up sorta wid one 'nudder atter dat, but dey wa'n't de gre't frien's dey wuz b'fo', en w'en it come t' frolics er argymints dey bofe uv'm 'uz allus on de udder side uv de fence f'um one 'nudder f'um dat time on twel now."

WHY SOME FOLKS IS BLACK EN SOME
IS WHITE

Aunt Betsey and Uncle Alford were talking. John came into the kitchen as Uncle Alford was saying: "Eve'y time Ah see dat nigger preacher, hit puts me in min' uv whut my daddy nuse t' say wuz de reason some folks 'uz white en some 'uz black."

He had finished his dinner. His plate was clean, except for a small piece of bread left for "manners"; now he was at peace with all the world—and Aunt Betsey, too.

Aunt Betsey turned to John, "Come on in hyere, Baby, you's jes in time—Brer Alfo'd's jes fixin' t' tell us 'bout how dat wuz."

"Aw-naw, Sis Betsey, not t'day," Uncle Alford said hurriedly, "Um's too plum full t' talk t'day, en 'sides dat, Ah done tole Big Man 'bout dat long 'fo' dis."

"Naw you ain't, Unc' Alfo'd," John said promptly and seriously, "Naw *suh*, you ain't, not never, never, *never*."

"Ah ain't?" Uncle Alford was surprised. "Well," he went on after a full minute's pause, "Ah'll ha' t' tell you dat tale 'fo' long—*sho*—en soon, too, but right now, Um got t'—"

"Fetch yo' cheer on over hyere by de fiahplace, Brer Alfo'd, so's Net en Henry Po'ter kin eat dey dinner," said Aunt Betsey. And then she added, "Whilest Um's waitin' fer dey dishes t' wash, you kin tell us 'bout it."

Uncle Alford followed her to the fireplace, chair in one hand and feeling in his pockets with the other. He put the chair down and then explored his pockets with both hands. They came out empty. "Ah wouldn' min' tellin' y'all 'bout dat, Sis Betsey, butchu *know* Ah jes cain' talk widout no—"

"I'll git you some, Unc' Alfo'd," said John gleefully. He knew by experience what was needed and was off like a shot.

The old man sat at one end of the hearth and Aunt Betsey sat at the other, while John, between them, on a stool at her feet, leaned against her knees and looked at Uncle Alford, eyes wide open.

Uncle Alford chewed appreciatively a minute or two and then began: "Well, when de Lawd fus' made de ye'th dar

wa'n't no sun ner no moon ner no stares ner nothin'—eve'y-
thing wuz dark—jes *black dark*—hit 'uz so dark you jes couldn'
see yo han' 'fo' yo' face, night ner day. En all de ye'th wuz
black, en de trees wuz black, en de watter wuz black, en w'en
He made de folkses he made dem black, too, 'ca'se He didn'
ha' nothin' t' make 'em out'n cep'm black dirt. En de folkses
didn' ha' no houses t' live in lak whut us is got now, dey
didn'; dey live' in caves in de side uv de mount'ns en in holes
dey dug in de hills en in ole holler logs; en eve'ywhar dey wuz,
hit wuz black, *plum black*.

"Atter while de folkses 'gun t' git tiah'd uv stumblin' roun'
all over eve'thing en stumpin' dey toes en runnin' into one
'nudder, en dey started axin' Gawd t' gi' 'em some he'p uv
some kin'. En de Lawd kep' puttin' 'em off, he did, en puttin'
'em off, 'ca'se He didn' jes zac'ly know whut t' do. De folkses
kep' atter 'im, dey did, en mos' nigh run 'im 'stracted, 'ntwel,
fus' en las', He call 'em all t'gedder one day en tole 'em He
'uz gwi gi' 'im de he'p dey been axin' fer, en ef dey didn' lak
whut He gi' 'em, dey jes ez well keep dey mouf shet, 'ca'se
He wa'n' gwi be worrit wid 'em no longer. De folkses 'uz
mighty glad, dey wuz, en dey ax 'im whut 'twuz he 'uz gwi
gi' 'em. Den he tole 'em dat de nex' day He 'uz gwi make de
sun fer'm, en he 'uz gwi make hit *soon* in de mo'nin', en dat
He wanted all uv 'em t' be dar bright en early en see him do it.

"Well, suh, dat night de folkses frolic roun' conside'ble, dey
did, en some uv 'em, spesh'ly dem whut 'uz sleepin' 'way in
de backside uv dem caves, overslep' deyse'fs. En Gawd got
mighty mad at 'em 'bout dat, he did, 'ca'se He done p'intedly
said fer'm t' be dar on time; so dem folkses whut 'uz on
time he made white en dem whut 'uz late he lef' black, en
he tole 'em, He did, dat ez long ez dey wuz so lazy en sleepy-
haided dat dey had t' ha' a bell ring t' wake 'em up on time
eve'y mo'nin', he wuz gwi make de white folks ring it; *en,*
dey been doin' it eve'y sence."

While Aunt Betsey and the old man were chuckling at this tale, John asked, "But Unc' Alfo'd, all black folks ain't plum black, is they?" And he turned questioning eyes from Henry's grinning, yellow face to Uncle Alford's.

Aunt Betsey's chuckle broke off in the middle—"Dar, Gawd," she said, and then, "Now whutchu gwi say?" she shot at Uncle Alford.

The old man was equal to the emergency and his chuckle was long and deep. "Um sho is glad you ax me 'bout dat, Big Man," he said, "dat's easy splained. You knows, uv co'se, dat some folks is blacker den de udders is, en some is brown en some is yaller?" John nodded his head. "Well, when Gawd made de sun, dem whut wuz sleepin' in de backside uv de caves didn' git no light a-tall en dey stayed black. But dem whut wuz closer t' de do' got mo' light, en dey wuz lighter-colored den whut dem on de backside uv de caves wuz, en de closer dey got t' de do' de lighter dey wuz, 'ntwel dem whut wuz sleepin' right in de do' mos' wuz yaller jes lak Henry. You see, don'chu?" he asked, and John nodded his head again—he saw!

WHEN BRER CRICKIT EN BRER FLEA
FELL OUT

Uncle Alford put the top on the box of shoe-blacking, brushed his hat with the shoe brush, and settled himself comfortably in his chair for a talk. "You 'members, Ah reggin, dat las' Sunday Ah tole you Ah wuz gwi tell you 'bout Brer Crickit en Brer Flea, en how dey come t' fall out wid one 'nudder; you 'members dat, don'chu?" he asked John.

"Yes suh, Unc' Alfo'd, en howcome a flea is little, too," answered the boy.

The old man chewed thoughtfully for a while; then clearing his throat, he spat 'way out to one side and began: "Yeah, dat's so. Well, suh, dat hap'm jes lak dis: Now Brer Flea wa'n't always de li'l bit a ha'r-hidin', back-bitin', hard-t'ketch somebody lak whut he is now, naw suh. In dem days he wuz a *big* man. Him en Brer Crickit wuz jes de same size. En dey bofe live in Mist' Man's h'a'th, right in front uv de fiahplace—one on one side uv a brick en de udder'n on de udder. En dey wuz gre't frien's in dem days en gre't singers, too. Brer Crickit, he sing p'utty much lak he do now, but Brer Flea had a big bass lak whut Brer Bullfrawg's is mos', en when dey went t' de Feas's in de Wilde'ness, en de Infairs en sociables, eve'y-body quit singin' when dey start en jes listen at dem. En when hit come t' de dancin'—Lawd, how dem two *could* *dance!* Dey do say dat dar wa'n't no two somebody's dat ever is been seed whut could cut de Pidgin Wing en Buzzu'd Lope lak whut dey could; en when dey dance de Double Shuffle, even ole Jedge Owul en Deakin Frawg, whut wuz bofe mighty 'ligious, dey wuz, nuse' t' pat fer'm en move dey foots roun' right bris' deyse'f—dey jes couldn' keep f'um it.

"Well, things would ha' kep' on bein' jes lak dat, dey would —eve'ybody havin' a good time—but Brer Flea wuz a devilish sorta pusson, he wuz, en kin' uv mean wid it, en w'en he see Brer Crickit talkin' t' some uv de gals he'd slip up behime 'em, he would, en bite 'em; en dey'd git mad en 'cuse Brer Crickit uv doin' it. At fus' dey'd laugh 'bout it a heap w'en dey 'uz gwine home, but Brer Flea got t' bitin' harder en harder 'ca'se he 'gun t' lak de tas'e uv it; en atter Brer Crickit done had two or three fights 'bout it, he tole Brer Flea dat he'd jes ha' to stop it. Brer Flea laugh, he did, en say he wouldn' do it no mo'. En dat *ve'y night* whilest Mist' Man wuz settin' in front uv de fiah en Brer Crickit wuz a-settin' on de h'a'th singin' jes loud ez he could, Brer Flea slip up, he did, en bit Mist' Man on de laig. Uv co'se Mist' Man wuz mad en he thought

Brer Crickit wuz into it, too. So he got up, he did, en th'owed some sulphur en red pepper in de fiah t' choke 'em, en den he po'd a bucket uv watter all over de h'a'th t' drown 'em, en he'd ha' kilt 'em bofe, too, he would, ef dey hadn' clum' up behime de mantle-she'f over de fiah.

"Atter Mist' Man went t' bed, Brer Crickit en Brer Flea 'gun t' qua'el, dey did, en fus' en las', w'en Brer Crickit 'cused Brer Flea uv bein' a no-mannered en a no-sense-ed fool en a liar wid it, dey fit. Man, suh, dey fit! Dey fit all over de house, dey did, en atter w'ile dey quit bitin' en scratchin' en went t' kickin'. Dey kick de san' f'um twix' de bricks in de h'a'th en to'e it up; den dey got in de chimbley en kick de mortar f'um twix' de bricks in de fiah-back, en dey fell out. Dey'd started kickin' de bricks out'n de front side uv de chimbley when Mist' Man got up en swo' he wuz gwi drown 'em dis time, en dey had t' run off en hide ag'in.

"Atter dat, eve'y time dey see one 'nudder, dey fit. Ef dey went t' chu'ch, dey fit en broke up de meetin'. When dey went t' de Feas' in de Wilde'ness, dey fit en broke up dat. Folkses had t' quit gi'n' dances 'ca'se dey'd break up eve'y one uv dem, sho. Ole Jedge Owul had 'em 'rested, he did, en foun' 'em, en Deakin Frawg, he chu'ched 'em, but still hit didn' do no good. Eve'ybody, mighty nigh, wuz mad wid 'em, en jes lak folkses will do, dey 'gun t' git mad at eve'ybody ilse deyse'f. Folkses 'gun t' wush dey'd kill one 'nudder en be done wid it.

"Fus' en las', Brer Crickit went t' see a ole witch-ooman whut wuz a frien' uv his'n en he tole her, he did, how de trouble twix' him en Brer Flea started. Den he tole her how dey done fit all over de house 'ntwel hit wa'n't no fittin' place t' live in; en he tole her 'bout how dey done fit en broke up de chu'ch meetin's; en how dey done fit en broke up de Feas's en de dances; en how eve'ybody wuz mad wid *him* when *he* hadn' done nothin' *a-tall,* en den he ax her t' he'p him git rid uv Brer Flea.

"De ole witch-ooman said she'd he'p 'im, but he'd ha' t' come back in a week er so, 'ca'se she had t' study 'bout whut she 'uz gwine do t' Brer Flea; en she say she know Brer Crickit didn' want Brer Flea kilt. En Brer Crickit 'low, he did, dat he wouldn' jes zac'ly say he wanted him *kilt,* but, still en all, ef Brer Flea *did* git kilt, he knowed good en well dat *he* wouldn' cry none, en dat sho wuz a fac'. Den de old witch-ooman say 'Aw right den,' en fer him t' come back nex' week.

"He come back, he did, dat ve'y nex' week, en de ole witch-ooman gi'n 'im a long, sharp, brass pin en tole 'im t' 'ten' lak he 'uz makin' frien's wid Brer Flea en t' git 'im t' bite a dawg fer'm; en when Brer Flea wuz bitin' de dawg he wuz t' stick dat pin in Brer Flea, en den jes watch. En dat's jes whut Brer Crickit done.

"When he got home, he knock on Brer Flea's do', en when Brer Flea come he say, he did, 'Brer Flea,' he say, 'dey ain't a bit a nuse in de worl' in us fightin' en gwine on no mo', lak whut us is been doin', en Ah jes come t' tell you dat ef you keep yo' mouf off'n me, Ah'll keep my mouf off'n you; en ef you keep yo' han's off'n me, Ah'll keep my han's off'n you. En dey ain't no reason den howcome us couldn' git along sorta lak us nuse to.' Den Brer Flea, he say, 'Aw right,' en dey shuck han's. En Brer Crickit, he 'lowed, he did, dat dar wuz one somebody dat he'd lak t' see bit, en bit good, en dat 'uz Mist' Man's ole blue-speckled houn' dawg whut 'uz sleepin' in front uv de fiah right den. When he said dat, Brer Flea pick his teeth wid one uv his sharp claws, he did, en he said, 'Come on.' Dey went up, dey did, t' whar Ole Blue wuz stretched out, en Brer Flea stuck his mouf in dem long ha'rs on his hind laig en tuck a big bite! Ole Blue flinch', he did, but didn' wake up, en Brer Flea, he hilt on. Den Brer Crickit step up, he did, en stuck dat pin in Brer Flea f'um behime en den he step back en watch. 'Nstidder gittin' bigger en bigger f'um all de blood he wuz suckin', Brer Flea started gittin' lit'ler en lit'ler, lit'ler en lit'ler, lit'ler en lit'ler, 'ntwel he went plum outa sight in dem ha'rs. Den dat ole blue houn' dawg got up en shuck hisse'f en trotted off, he did, en tuck Brer Flea wid 'im; en, f'um dat day t' dis, Brer Crickit ain't been worrit a bit wid Brer Flea no mo'."

DAWGS IS MIGHTY KNOWIN' THINGS

H-y-e-r-e, Hero, h-y-e-r-e, hyere, hyere. Peter, howcome you reggin dat dawg don' come on? Wunner ef he at de kitchen?" So, at a dead run, Henry Porter and John started for the house. Aunt Betsey met them at the kitchen door with: "Whut's you chillun done foun' now?"

Henry caught his breath first and answered, "Us seed a rabbit in de tater patch! Whar Hero at? Dar he, right behime Ai' Betsey! Come on hyere, dawg! Is you deef?" But Hero, usually anxious for a chase or frolic, plainly didn't want to go. They were puzzled at his behavior; he would just stand and look at Aunt Betsey—his tail and head drooping—a picture of dejection.

"Take 'im 'long wid you, Honey," Aunt Betsey said uneasily, "He been lookin' at me lak dat sence way 'fo' dinner, en hit's makin' me feel cu'us, hit do."

Said Aunt Emily, from beside the fireplace: "Dawgs is

mighty knowin' things, Sis Betsey. Dey knows a heap a things dey cain' tell, en dey knows 'em 'fo' us do. Ah been wun'rin' 'bout dat dawg—"

"Ah been wun'rin' 'bout 'im too," said Aunt Betsey. "'Tain't nachel fer dat dawg t' do dattaway—he all de time bris' in 'is ways."

"Yeah, dat's so, en Ah boun'ju you gwi hyeah—," but the boys didn't wait to learn what was going to be heard. Henry had got Aunt Emily's calf-rope from the dairy near by, and, with that tied around Hero's neck, they were dragging him to the chase. When they were almost to the potato patch, they had to stop to rest. Hero rested too, sitting on his haunches and looking at first one and then the other with no show of interest.

"Now jes look at dat ole dawg, Peter," said Henry disgustedly, "jes *look* at 'im, won'chu? He ain't a bit a 'count!"

"He is, too! Dat's a good dog, Hero is, an' you know it."

"A good dawg? Huh! Howcome he ain' come he'p us ketch dat rabbit, den? Howcome he ain' do dat?"

"I spec' he's hungry, Henry."

"Hongry? Shucks! You didn' see 'im w'en he et his dinner, didju? Net, she gi'n 'im a pan *full* an' Ah gi'n 'im part uv mines too, en now, atter *all dat,* yere he is won' go ketch dat rabbit fer us. Ah done plum gi'n out wid him, Ah is."

"But, Henry," said John, still hunting excuses for Hero's behavior, "maybe you give him too much dinner. That's what's the matter, his stomach's hurtin' him."

"Naw, 'tain't, Peter, dawgs don' ha' no bellyache. You know dat. 'Sides, ef he did ha' it, whyn't he lie down en roll over lak a mule do?"

"'Cause he ain't a mule," said John, defensively.

"Don' kyere ef he ain't, he got fo' feets, ain't 'e?"

This reasoning being unanswerable, John jumped up and started for the potato patch on the run. Hero was surprised into following them, and in a few minutes they were joined by two more dogs from the quarters that had been attracted by the noise. The hunt was on. Presently, the eager yelping of the dogs announced that a rabbit had been jumped and Henry's "Da' he! Da' he! Gittim! Whoo-e, y-o-n 'e go, y-o-n 'e go! *ketch'im,* dawg!" indicated that the chase was hot. One of the dogs from the quarters was in the lead and gaining fast, the other one was second, and Hero, too fat for speed, was a poor third. "*Look at dat yaller pup,* Pe-tuh-huh! Jes lookit 'im!" yelled Henry. "He runnin' sideways jes t' keep f'um flyin! 'At's a *dawg* 'e is! *Gwon,* pup!"

The rabbit was lost in the brushes and weeds of "de big ditch," but not for long. The boys took opposite sides of the ditch, and each tried to keep the "yaller pup" with him. Soon came Henry's quick "Yere'e! Yere'e! Hyere! Hyere! Ketch 'im! He on yo' side, Peter, watch 'im!" Henry and all the dogs crossed over together and the tired cottontail was caught. Henry rushed up to the dog that had already started to eat it. "Put 'im *down, dawg,* 'fo' Ah bus' yo' haid wide op'm!" He handed the rabbit to John: "You kin tote 'im, Peter, but pull 'is tail off fus'."

"What for?"

"Gimme quick w'ile 'e hot," and Henry proceeded hurriedly to pull off the cottony tuft that gives the rabbit its most familiar name. "You ha' t' do dat ef you wants t' ketch any mo'," he explained. "Now us gwi git anudder'n."

They hunted until time to go for the cows but found nothing. John was willing to blame Henry for that. "Thought us was goin' t' ketch another one, Henry?"

"Us would'a, but us didn' *fin'* narry un."

"I know us didn'," said John, "but you said us 'ud ketch another one when you pulled this tail off," and he held it out to Henry accusingly.

"M-y L-a-w-d, Peter! En you picked hit up! Ah knowed sump'm wuz de matter. Ah p'intedly pull dat rabbit's tail off en th'owed hit away fer luck, en yere you come en pick us luck up en put 'tin yo' pockit! Gawd knows us ain' gwi *nevuh* ketch nothin' ef you gwi do dattaway."

Henry had put John on the defensive. "Shucks! I don't b'lieve it. Pullin' his tail off don' do no good."

"Yeh, hit do, Peter," Henry said commiseratingly, "Yeh hit do, ef you th'ows hit away, hit do. But ef you don' th'ow hit away you jes ez well let hit stay whar hit wuz at. Ef you th'ows hit away, all de udder rabbits see hit en know sump'm done hap'm t'im, en dey gits skeered en skittish en jump up quick so you kin see 'em, 'nstidder hidin' good. Dat's de way dey do, en ef you don' b'lieve me, you kin ax Ai' Betsey, er Ai' Em'ly, er Unc' Harry, er Unc' Shed, er Unc' Aaron, er *any*body. All de ole folks say dat, en you know dey knows, de ole folks do." This array of testimony was overwhelming. "Hit sho look lak Ah cain' l'arn you nothin'," he went on, "you didn' wan' t' swolly dat fish bladder en you couldn' swim a lick, couldju? Well, you did swollit, en now you kin swim cross de creek mos' good ez Ah kin, cain'chu? You didn' b'lieve me w'en Ah tole you you'd git some new clo's ef you bite dat butterfly's haid off, didju? Well Ah worrit wid you mos' all day twel you done it, didn' Ah? En now Miss Sallie done tole Mars John she gwi git you a blue su'ge suit come Chris'mus, ain' she?"

"Whut's su'ge, Henry?" asked John, trying to stop this recitation of his shortcomings.

"Don' know whut 'tis, but hit's p'utty. En you wouldn' spit on yo' fishbaits 'fo' you th'owed hit in de creek twel you see Ah cotch mos' all de fishes, en now, you ketch jes ez many ez Ah does. You sho is hard t' l'arn, Peter, but dey's one thing sho—Ah ain' gwine huntin' wid you no mo' ef you don' pull de rabbit's tail off en th'ow 'em away, 'ca'se d'aint no use huntin' ef you ain' gwi ketch nothin', en you know dat."

"Well, I'll do it after dis," John said, thoroughly convinced now, and, as a proof of sincerity, he threw away the tail that he still held.

The boys looked for Hero to go to the pasture with them, but he was nowhere to be found. In disgust, they finally quit calling him, and Henry suggested that John "take dat rabbit en show Miss Sallie whut us cotch, en you fetch in de stove wood fer me, but don' le' nobody skin it 'ca'se us got t' do dat usse'f."

When John reached the kitchen, he heard Aunt Betsey's and Aunt Emily's low worried tones. "Sis Em'ly, dat dawg—jes look at 'im. Sump'm gwi hap'm, sho."

"Ah know hit is, Sis Betsey, but whut? Dat's whut Ah wants t' know—en who to? Dawgs is mighty knowin' critters, dey is. Is you feelin' well t'day, Sis Betsey?"

"Middlin' well, Sis Em'ly, middlin'. Howcome you ast me dat?"

"Well, Sis Betsey, dawgs is mighty knowin' things, dey is, en Ah wuz jes wun'rin'—"

John managed to make himself heard, but had to be insistent. "Ai' Betsey, look-a-here! Look whut us caught."

"Bless Gawd, ef dat chile ain' cotch a rabbit. Whyn't chu wait'll fall fer dat, Honey? Rabbits ain' no good dis time uv de yeah—not twel frost come en 'simmons is ripe—dey ain't." John started to protest, but she broke in with: "All right, den, you skin 'im en Ah'll cook 'im ef dey ain' no wolves in 'is back. Ef dey is, you'll ha' t' gi' 'im to Hero." Then suddenly remembering Hero—"Take 'im on out'n hyere, won'chu, Baby? Supper ought t' be half done en my stove ain' good hot. Whutchu reggin make 'im look so sor'ful-lak?"

"Dawgs is mighty knowin' things, Ai' Betsey," said John, parrot-like, "you know dat."

"*Whut's dat?* Listen t' 'im, Sis Em'ly! Whut's dat means, Baby! Tell mammy," she coaxed.

Tickled at the impression he was making, John dropped

into the mysterious tones she often used to him: "Sorrow an' death when dey howls, Ai' Betsey," he said.

"D'ju hyeah dat, Sis Em'ly?" she asked, her voice low and trembling. Aunt Betsey dropped into a chair, for her knees had given away. " 'Out'n de mouvs uv babes—' Lawd," she cried, casting her eyes upward. "Who hit gwi be dis time? Is it me, Lawd?"

"Ah don' spec' hit kin be you, Sis Betsey," said Aunt Emily, soothingly, "You's still feelin' middlin' well, ain'chu?"

"Only toler'ble, Sis Em'ly. Dis mo'nin' Ah foun' a big pin in de path wid de haid twoge me. Ah made a cross mark 'fo' Ah pick it up, Ah did, en th'owed hit over my lef' shoulder, en now Ah 'members a ole black cat cross my path gwine sorta norf-lak. En den dis e'nin' dat daid tree at de cow lot fell w'en Ah wuz at de woodpile. Dar wa'n't no win' blowin', needer, but Ah didn' think nothin' 'bout dat den. Dat's a sign uv death, Sis Em'ly, you know dat."

"Hit sho is, Sis Betsey, hit sholy is," admitted Aunt Emily.

"En now," went on Aunt Betsey, "dat dawg been tryin' t' tell me sump'm all *day*. Lawd," her voice was trembling, "you is tried t' warn me, en Ah ain' listen."

"Maybe hit ain't *you*, Sis Betsey," said Aunt Emily, "you is feelin' toler'ble well, ain'chu?"

"No'm, Ah ain't, Sis Em'ly, hit's wuss'n dat. Ah's got a powerful mis'ry in my chis' en hit's hu'tin' me mighty bad right now, hit is. Call Net fer me," she said feebly, "Um gwi git her t' finish gittin' supper fer me, Ah jes ain' able. Ah ain' ready t' go, Lawd," she prayed, looking skyward.

"Aw yes you is, Sis Betsey, Ah knows better'n dat."

"Ah ought t' be, yes, Ah ought t' be but Ah ain't, Ah's done backslid. Ah wuz singin' a reel fer Baby jes yistiddy en showin' 'im sorta how us nuse t' dance. But Ah didn' cross my feets, Lawd, you 'member dat, please," she pleaded.

Aunt Emily tried to be consoling. "Ah keep a-thinkin' 'bout

dat dawg; look at 'im good, Sis Betsey. He ain' sorry *fer* you; he sorry *at* you."

"Dat is so!" said Aunt Betsey, brightening up a little.

"Whichaway wuz dat pin p'intin'? asked Aunt Emily.

"Sorta norf en wes'," Aunt Betsey answered.

"Now you see dar? En whichaway dat tree fall?"

"Sorta norf en wes' too. But whut dat got t' do wid it, Sis Em'ly?"

"Lawd, Honey, Ah spec's dat's de way de trouble comin' f'um; dat's sho de way hit p'ints. Now us got t' wait twel dat dawg howls en see whichaway he's p'intin'. Us'll be sho, den."

"But you listen, Sis Em'ly," wailed Aunt Betsey, "Ah ain't tole you all uv it yit 'ca'se Ah jes 'membered. Yistiddy e'nin' a peckerwood lit on my house en pecked, he did, twel Ah th'owed fus' a knife en den a fock at 'im. Dat's a sign uv death, you know dat. But Ah didn' pay hit no min' den. En las' night a scrich owul sot on m' chimbley en hollered 'ntwel Ah th'owed a han'ful uv salt in de fiah en den Ah had t' put de shevel in too, 'fo' he'd go 'way. Dat's a sign uv death, too, but Ah didn' pay hit no min', needer. You know dat's a sign, don'chu, Sis Em'ly?"

"Dat's so, Sis Betsey, dat is sholy so." Aunt Emily felt almost as much frightened now as was Aunt Betsey—but there was more to come.

"En dis mo'nin'," she went on, "Ah foun' sump'm at m' gate all wrapped up in red flannin en tied wid a piece uv cowhide—skin uv some kin' hit wuz, anyways. Ah tuck it up in de shevel en th'owed hit in de fiah en burnt it up, en hit jes sizzled, hit did. Ah done wrong w'en Ah done dat—Ah knows hit now."

"Ooman," said Aunt Emily in a subdued tone, "you made a *mis*take dat time, sho! Howcome you didn' beh'y it in de focks uv de path? Ef you'd a done dat en put three grains uv black pepper, some asfedity, en a ingon-button wid it, it 'ud sho th'owed de chahm back on de one 'at put it dar jes ez soon's dey step over it."

"Ah knows hit now, Sis Em'ly, but—Lawd," she moaned, "atter dis, ef you spares me dis time, Ah'll sho pay 'tention t' yo' signs, Lawd."

Aunt Emily made a practical suggestion: "Git Net t' fix supper fer you en you go see Sis Polly en git 'er t' gi' you sump'm t' he'p you; she do dat easy. En w'ile you gone, ef dat dawg howls Ah'll see 'im, sho."

Hero was tied to the chinaberry tree at the dairy so that Aunt Emily could keep her eye on him. Net started supper and Aunt Betsey went to Aunt Polly for much needed help. She came back shortly in a little better frame of mind—but not much better. Supper was late, of course, and Mars John, having learned the reason while Aunt Betsey was consulting Aunt Polly, was walking up and down the front porch, fretting and threatening to "put a stop to this damn nigger foolishness once and for all."

When he heard Aunt Betsey's voice in the kitchen again, he charged that stronghold with: "Betsey, what sort of foolishness are you up to now, throwing everything late like this? I'm not going to have it, and you know it."

"Oh, Mars John," cried the old woman, "hit ain' foolishness, dis time! Jes listen en le' me tell you." Then followed a detailed recitation of the happenings of the past two days, ending with, "En you knows dem signs well ez me, Mars John, en hit means me er my chillun."

Her distress was very genuine, he could see that. "Signs fail lots of times, Betsey," he said kindly, "you know that."

"One sign does, Ah knows, but how kin *all uv'm* fail to onest, Mars John? How kin dey do dat? Jes tell me?"

"Well," he said, "I know there's nothing wrong at the home place because I saw Robert at the post office this evening, and he said everybody was well. Now I know signs—you know I do—and it looks like whatever is going to happen has already happened. So it can't be you or any of the children or we would have heard before now. Besides that, the signs don't point here nor to the home place, but northwest, and you haven't anybody in the northwest to worry about. Don't it look that way to you, Emily?"

"Hit sho do, Mars John, hit sho do look jes dattaway, lak Ah been tellin' Sis Betsey. 'Sides dat, dat dawg ain' howl yit, en twel he do, us won' know ef it's a death howl er ilse a moon howl. Us'll ha' t' wait fer dat."

Supper was soon over, the dishes were washed, and things made ready for morning. Aunt Betsey stayed until the kitchen was darkened. Hero was still silent. On Mars John's promise to see which way the dog was pointing if he howled before bedtime, and to tell her, Aunt Betsey went home, still uneasy and still "wid a tech uv mis'ry in de chis'."

Later, curled up at his uncle's feet, little John asked him how he could tell a "moon howl" from a "death howl." "Well, son," he said, "I can't tell one howl from another by the sound, but the negroes say it's a 'moon howl' when the dog points his nose at the moon—that doesn't mean anything much. But when he looks away from the moon and howls, they think that news of death is sure to come from the direction the dog's nose is pointing. But you look here, suh, don't you get to believing any such 'nigger foolishness' as that. I'll make you stay away from 'em if you do."

But Auntie said, "Let him alone, John. If he does believe it now, he'll get over it just as you did. You know," she laughed at him, "you used to believe in 'ha'nts' and witches, and just such 'nigger foolishness' as that."

John protested that he didn't believe in anything like that "a-tall." But he did, for Aunt Betsey's teachings were firmly rooted.

Soon it was late bedtime, and little John backed up to his

uncle and leaned forward to act as his bootjack (a treasured privilege), when on the night there rose a sound—long, loud, and dismal—a sound that no combination of words or letters can really describe. "Ah-h-oo-oo-oo-" it started low down on the bass clef and gradually reached the highest note known in "dogdom." Then it eased back to lower notes and ended almost as low as it started, "-oo-oo-oo-ah." It was clear and musical, but depressing. "By Golly! What a whopper!" said Mars John. He started for the back yard, and little John hung a hand in his uncle's coat pocket and went too. Hero opened up again just as they got there. He was sitting on his haunches with his back toward Aunt Betsey's house and his nose to the northwest. "Hi, Betsey!" Mars John called, "pointing northwest, ole lady. Now go t' sleep."

"Thankee, Mars John," she answered, "thankee, suh. Ah mos' knowed hit wuz gwi be somwhar ilse."

"Do you hear that old liar, son?" he laughed, looking at John.

Mars John's place, where many of the old family negroes lived, *was* actually northwest of them. Although they generally spoke of it as north.

Back in his room Mars John said, "Sallie, I wonder if anything can be wrong up there?"

" 'Nigger foolishness,' John," she mocked. "Sonny Boy," to little John, "don't you get to believing any such 'nigger foolishness' as that."

"Shucks! Sallie," was all that Mars John could say and he went to bed.

The next morning one of her boys, Robert, brought Aunt Betsey news of the birth and death of a grandchild.

"Ah mos' knowed sump'm 'uz gwi hap'm," she said, "en Ah didn' rightly think hit could be me. Ah wa'n't skeered fer m'se'f, dough," she went on, "'ca'se all my priperations done been made fer yeahs, en ef de Lawd had a call me, Ah wuz ready en willin' t' go. You know dat, Sis Em'ly. But Ah *wuz* skeered 'bout my chilluns, Ah wuz dat."

"Sho, sho," agreed Aunt Emily, but on the way to the dairy she chuckled knowingly.

GHOS'ES

Ai' Betsey," asked John, "is they any ghos'es?"

John knew, of course, that there were ghosts—the world was full of them; but when Aunt Betsey talked of "sperrits en sich" he would ask her this to confirm his own belief.

"Whutchu talkin' 'bout, Honey? Does you mean is dey any ha'nts?"

"Yes'm. Net say ghos'es en ha'nts de same. Dey ain't, is dey, Ai' Betsey?"

"Well," she admitted after pondering thoughtfully, "dey mout be en den ag'in dey moutn't. You see, Honey, ghos'es is ghos'es, en ha'nts is ha'nts, en dey is a diff'unce. Ah gwi tell you 'bout dat sometime. Whut make you ax me dat?"

"Net, she say heap a folks kin see 'em. Unc' Harry, he kin see 'em; Ai' Em'ly, she kin see 'em; Unc' Shed, he kin see 'em; an' Ai' Polly, she—"

"Net tell you 'bout Sis Polly seein' 'em?" She looked rather grave now.

"Yes'm."

"When she say she see de las' un?"

"She say Ai' Polly see 'em a heap a times. Kin you see 'em, Ai' Betsey?" he asked eagerly. "You kin, cain't you?"

"No-o-o," she replied slowly. When John's disappointment showed in his face, she added, "Dat is, not much, not now. You see, Baby, hit's dissaway. Sperrits ain' bothered me much uv late yeahs, not much, dey ain't; not sence Ah got 'ligion. En 'sides dat, Ah done l'arnt how t' keep 'em off."

"How you do it, Ai' Betsey? Is you got a buckeye, er a sperrit-bone, er a—"

"Nemmine 'bout dat now," she interrupted, "Um gwi tell you 'bout dat sometimes when you gits bigger. You don' ha' t' know now, 'ca'se ha'nts don' nevuh git atter li'l chillun, dat is, good li'l chillun. You's good, ain'chu?"

John wasn't the least bit modest or bashful about admitting it.

"Well, you all right den," she said. "Now Um's got t' wash dese hyere supper dishes, 'ca'se Ah wants t' git home 'fo' hit's dark en dat ain't gwine to be long. Whar John de Baptis'?"

But John's mind was on ghosts, not on pet chickens. "He's sleep in de henhouse, Ai' Betsey." And then in a mysterious whisper, "Us goin' t' see Ai' Polly t'night. Ain'chu goin' wid us?"

"Who's gwine wid you?"

"Me an' Net an' Henry Po'ter."

"Naw, Baby, Um's got some sewin' t' do en Ah cain' go t'night. Don'chu le'm skeer you now."

Later she cautioned Net: "Don' let dat boy git skeered t'night, gal. You watch dat."

Net told Mars John and Miss Sallie where they wanted to go, and they gave their permission. Mars John also gave little John the "chaw uv 'bac'er" for Aunt Polly that he had been told to ask for.

Aunt Polly was old, old—by her own statement, "Gawd hisse'f is de onliest one whut knows how ole Ah reely is." And she looked it. Her hair was very gray for a Negro, and most of her teeth were gone. She was "toler'ble spry, dough, en able t' git roun' conside'ble."

After making them welcome and asking separately after the health of everyone at "de big house," she wanted to know, "Whar y'all gwine dis time a night?" Net said, "Us come t' see you, Ai' Polly. Baby, he wan' t' hyeah 'bout some ha'nts."

"Which'en?"

"De one dat at de cow lot, Ai' Polly. Unc' Harry said he seed him. You know 'bout that'n don'chu?" John asked anxiously.

"Does Ah? But chu look heah, Ain't none uv y'all thought to fetch me nothin'?"

"Yes'm, I did. I brought you some 'bac'er, Ai' Polly. Here hit." John left Net's side long enough to hand it to her, and with an expectant shiver shrank back against Net's arm.

"Dat's right, dat's right. Mustn't fergit de old folks. Boy!" she snapped at one of her grandchildren, "Does Ah ha' t' tell you *all* de time whut t' do? *Gimmypipe!*"

Aunt Polly crushed the tobacco in her hand and filled her pipe carefully, all the time looking intently in the fire. The piece of kindling put on when the children came in had burned up, and now the only light that lit the semicircle of black faces and John's came from an occasional little blaze that flared up from the half-burnt log that lay on a big bed of live coals. "Does Ah know 'bout dat sperrit at de lot? *Ah does.*" Her voice sank to a low monotone. "Hit happened jes dissaway. A long, long time ago, hit wuz—way back in slave'y time 'fo' anybody whut's on dis place now wuz livin', dat is, 'ceptin' me, en Ah wuz jes a young gal.

"Dar wuz a white man whut own de place en all de niggers, en he wuz a mighty good man to his niggers too, he wuz, twel he got drunk en den he wuz mean, *mean*. One mo'nin' he yelled de folks up 'way 'fo' day en tole 'em t' git to de woods en cut en hew some logs, he wuz gwine buil' a house, en fer dem t' huh'y er he'd come down dar in de woods en huh'y 'em. En Tom—whut wuz my daddy—wuz de overseer, en he tole 'em all dey better huh'y 'ca'se Marster wuz gittin' drunk en dey knowed whut dat means. In mos' no time, de niggers had de logs uppit de yard en he made 'em buil' a li'l house wid no winders. En w'ile dey wuz buildin' hit, he'd take a cut at fus' one en den de udder, en w'en dey holler he'd jes laugh en go t' de house en git anudder drink. He kep' 'em at it, he did, all day en all night, en nex' day jes 'bout dinner time hit wuz th'ough. Den de man say, 'You don' know whut dat is, do you?' En dey all say, 'Naw suh,' 'ca'se dey did'n'. 'Well,' he say, 'hit's my jail-house, en de fus' one whut gits in hit gwi wish de devul had 'em.' En den he made Tom take a long spike en drive it in de tree nex' t' de jail-house, en den he says, 'Dat's fer some uv you, too.'" Aunt Polly lowered her voice impressively, "An dat's de same jail-house whut's up in de yard, and dat same spike's in de same tree, en you kin see it right now ef you look.

"Now the Marster had a nigger man name Jim. He had anudder name, too, whut his daddy, whut wuz a Affiken Cunjer man, gi' 'im, but us couldn' say dat—nobody could— so eve'y body call him Jim fer short. En Jim wuzn't lak de udder folks. He didn' talk en cah'y on wid de res' uv'm, jes sorta mumble to hisse'f en sing to hisse'f a song whut nobody knowed whut wuz about. En he didn' go to chu'ch come Sundays, lak eve'body ilse done; jes went out in de woods, he did, en ramble about en talk to hisse'f. En w'en my daddy ax 'im howcome dat wuz, he jes look at 'im hard a minute en didn' bat 'is eye, en he said, he did, 'Gawd out dar,' en he p'inted t' de woods, 'not dar,' en he p'inted t' de chu'ch. En den he walk off, he did, en my daddy say 'is eyes made him feel funny, en he didn' ax 'im no mo'.

"One day atter dat, some boys en gals wuz out in de woods a-pickin' up scaly-barks, en dey come 'cross Jim, settin' on a hollow log, he wuz, en he had a buckeye in one han' en a bone—folks' bone, hit wuz, too—in de udder un, en he wuz talkin' to 'em, *en dey wuz talkin' back to him*. Dey run home, dey did, en tell de folks, 'ca'se dey wuz skeered, en atter dat de folkses let Jim alone 'ca'se dey wuz skeered, too."

The light from the dying coals had got dim. Aunt Polly spat in the fire, and the "plop," followed by a faint frying sound, made John jump, and then shrink closer to Net. One of the children threw on a little chip, but the blaze didn't last long, and afterward the room seemed darker than ever. A falsetto-voiced cricket squeaked impatiently to a lagging mate. For a minute there was no other sound but breathing. Then, leaning over, the old woman took a pinch of ashes from the hearth, held them on her left palm, and blew them toward the fire and watched them settle. Out in the skirt of woods back of the house a screech owl sent out his quivering call. "Listen!" Aunt Polly said, holding up her hand. In a minute the owl was answered by another, this time nearer the house.

"De signs say dey's walkin' t'night." With a shudder John thought of the darkness between him and the "big house" and safety, and wished he were at home.

"Well," she continued, raising her voice, "de ve'y nex' day atter de jail-house wuz finished, Marster wuz drinkin' wuss'n ever, en he had de niggers cuttin' wood at de woodpile 'ca'se hit rain endurin' de night en hit 'uz too wet to pick cotton.

"En lak Ah said, de Marster-man wuz drinkin' wuss'n ever, en he wuz a-cussin' en a-blackgyardin' 'em all de time but he hadn' hit none uv 'em yit.

"Atter w'ile Jim stop a minute, he did, en sorta le'nt on 'is axe-handle 'ca'se he'd been wuckin' hard en fas' en his win' gin out. De Marster-man he say, 'Jim!' right short-lak. Eve'ybody jump cep'm Jim, en he say 'Suh?' En den de Marster-man ax 'im whut dat wuz in 'is pockit, en he say, 'Fedder.'

" 'Whar you git it?'

"Jim say he foun' it, an de Marster-man tole 'im t' fetch it to 'im. Den he say, 'Dat's a green fedder, en you didn' fin' it. You been stealin' my chickens, ain'chu?'

"Jim say, 'Naw Suh.'

"'Don' you lie t' me. You stole my chickens didn'chu? Huh?'

"'Naw, Suh, Ah ain' stole nothin',' Jim say, en den de ole Marster-man got so mad de slobber 'gin t' run out'n 'is mouf.

"'You steal my chickens an den 'spute my word. Um gwi fix you fer dat.' En den he made Tom, my daddy, take a plow-line en tie 'is han's t'gedder en th'ow de udder en' over dat spike en pull on it twel Jim's feet jes tech de groun'. En den he tuck en whup 'im twel he tiah'd, en den he say, 'Stole my chickens, didn'chu?' En when Jim say, 'Naw, Suh,' he git madder'n ever en start whuppin' 'im ag'in en he say all de time he whuppin' 'im, 'Steal my chickens.' Whack! 'Lie to me.' Whack! ''Spute my word.' Whack! En Jim don' beg ner nothin'—jes' moan-lak t' hisse'f, en you could see de meat on 'is back quiverin' 'ca'se de whup done cut 'is shu't all off 'im. En den he made de udder niggers th'ow 'im in de jail-house, en den he went t' de big house hisse'f en drink some mo'.

"Dat wuz jes about a hour by sun. Jes 'fo' sundown he made 'em bring Jim out, en' he say he gwi make 'im tell de trufe 'bout dat fedder, ef he kill 'im. En den he made 'em pull 'im up t' de spike ag'in. At de ve'y fus' lick he hit 'im, de rope slip off de spike en Jim he break en run, de rope draggin' en de Marster-man tryin' t' ketch 'im en cuttin' at 'im all de time wid de whup. En Jim he run t' de cow lot en clum' de fence wid de Marster-man right atter 'im. En he run in one en' uv de cow shed en out de udder, en den he clum' de fence ag'in en made a circle roun' whar de henhouse is now, and den de Marster-man, he step on de rope whut wuz draggin' en th'owed Jim on 'is face en he run up, he did, en kick en stomp 'im sump'm awful. Den he tole de udders t' take 'im back en pull 'im up. Dey done it, en de Marster cut 'im once en drawed back fer anudder lick, when Jim he say, 'You done now, Marster. T'morrow night! T'morrow night!' He said it

"De Marster-man say, 'Jim, wake up, Jim!'"

twice, jes dattaway, en den his knees gin 'way en he jes hung dar. De Marster-man thought a minute en drap de whup, en den he laugh sorta funny-lak, he did, en he say, 'He-he! Jim sleep,' en he look lak he jes woke up hisse'f.

"He tole de udder folks t' untie 'im, but dey couldn' git de knot loose, so he tole em t' cut de rope. Dey cut hit, dey did, en Jim fell down all crumpled up lak en gi'n one groan, en jes den two scrich owuls flew f'um out de tree twoge de big house, en lit, one on one chimbley en one on de udder. De Marster-man say, 'Jim, wake up, Jim!' Jim didn' say nothin', en den he put 'is han' on Jim en shuck 'im. En he laugh kinda funny ag'in, he did, en put his han' un'er 'im en try t' lif' 'im, en den he look up at Tom, sorta s'prise'-lak, en say, 'He wet.' He look at 'is han's terreckly en see dey red, en den right quick he wa'n't drunk no mo'. He look at 'em ag'in, he did, kinda hard, en den he sorta whisper-lak, 'Hit's blood,' he sez. 'Hit's blood. Hit's blood.' He look twoge de sun, en you could jes see de aige uv it, en say, 'Hit's down now—red, too.' Den he went t' de house, steppin' careful en easy, lak he didn' wan' t' make no fuss. Jes 'fo' he git t' de house de scrich owul, whut wuz on de chimbley twoge de jail, gi'n a li'l low moan, en he stop sho't-lak en say, 'Datchu, Jim?' Den he look up, en 'g'inst de sky he see dat scrich owul settin' on de chimbley, en he stood still en 'gun t' shake. Den he went t' de kitchen en made de cook go light de lamp in 'is room, en call Tom, my daddy.

"When Tom come, he say, 'Whar he?'

"En Tom say, 'He out un'er de tree jes lak he wuz.'

"'Ain' move?' he ast 'im. En w'en he say, 'Naw, suh,' den he tole 'im t' take kyere uv 'im.

"Now dat wuz on de Sa'day 'fo' de las' Sunday in October.

"Well, dey moved Jim t' his house en dressed 'im en put ashes over de blood at de foot uv de tree, en de nex' day dey beh'ied 'im.

"Dat night de Marster-man wouldn' let Ole Tom go home,
but he made 'im stay uppit de house wid him. Tom he set in
de chimbley cornder en Marster he rock in 'is big cheer en
smoke en sorta nod-lak. 'Long twoge midnight de owul hollered ag'in, en he jumped up, he did, en tole Tom t' come on.
Daddy said he wuz skeered t' go an skeered not to. He foll'ed
'im jes a li'l ways behime, en w'en he got close, he seed de
Marster-man wuz leanin' over sump'm on de groun' at de foot
uv de tree en wuz tuggin' at it lak he wuz tryin' t' lif' it. En
w'en he got up t' de tree de thing whut he seed on de groun'
wuz gone. Lak dat! Jes gone! En de Marster-man stood up en
wuz feelin' all his fingers wid 'is thumbs, en he said, 'He wet,'
jes lak dat. En ole Tom, my daddy, led 'im in t' de house, en
all de way he hilt 'is han's in front uv 'im en teched all 'is
fingers wid 'is thumbs, en kep' a-sayin', 'He wet. He wet.'
An' w'en he got t' de light he look at 'is han's en dey all
bloody. Den he made Tom git some watter en some soap en
he wash, en wash, en wash, but hit don' come off. En he look
at 'em en look at Tom en den he say sof' en easy-lak, 'Whut
kin Ah do?' En Tom didn' say nothin' 'ca'se he didn' know.
Jes den dat ole scrich owul out on de chimbley gi'n a laugh,
a long laugh, hit wuz, en he laugh low en he laugh loud. En
de Marster-man he sorta crumple up by 'is cheer en he look
jes lak Jim did, my daddy say, 'ca'se his han's wuz hilt straight
up lak Jim's wuz, en t'gedder, en he say, 'O Gawd'lmighty,
will dey be lak dis all de time? Won't hit never come off? I
cain't ax fer much mussey Lawd, Ah know Ah cain't, but
fer jes a li'l w'ile take hit away, Lawd, fer jes a li'l w'ile.' En
he jes shuck. 'Hyeath me, Gawd,' he say, 'hyeah me. Ah cain't
see blood *all* de time.' He ain't pray loud, jes whisp'rin'-lak.
En Tom he say low jes lak Marster doin', 'Oh hyeah him,
Jesus, hyeah him!' En dey pray lak dat, fus' one pray en den
de udder. En den Marster say, 'Lemme wash hit off fer a li'l
w'ile, Jesus.' En dat wuz de fus' time he call Jesus' name.

"Den Tom, my daddy, say out *loud*, 'Wash 'is han's in Yo' blood, Jesus, en hyeah 'im.' But Marster he holler, 'No! Fer Gawd's sake, not dat! Not dat! No! No blood, Jesus, but jes a li'l mussey!' Den right quick he say, 'Thank You, Jesus,' en he stood up en look at 'is han's en my daddy stood up en look at 'em, en de blood wuz all gone. Marster tuck en lay down cross de bed en he sleep in a minute. En daddy Tom look out de winder en see day wuz breakin'. Dey had prayed all night!

"Well," Aunt Polly continued in a new tone that was a relief from the low, steady, dreadful monotony of the other. "Atter dat, things went along jes 'bout de same as usual, dat is, in de daytime. De Marster drink a li'l along but he don' whup de niggers no mo'. But come dark, he git up en look at 'is han's en den walk out t' de woodpile, en de jail-house, en de tree, en de cow shed, en t' whar de henhouse is, en back, en t' de tree ag'in, en mos' all de time one uv dem owuls foll' 'im. En w'en he come t' de house, he look at 'is han's ag'in en he say, 'Hit's jes fer a li'l w'ile.'

"Atter dat he nevuh put 'is lamp out at night, en jes one week f'um de night Jim died, eve'y limb on dat side uv de tree wuz daid en ain' none nevuh grow back dar no mo'.

"De nex' Sa'day atter Jim die, late in de e'enin', Marster was gi'n out rations en Tom, my daddy, whut wuz de meat-cutter en de weigher, say, 'Dat's all.' En Marster count en say, 'Dey's one mo',' en w'en Tom say, 'Ev'ybody got dey'n, Marster,' he say, sorta snappy-lak, 'Dey's one mo', Ah tells you. Git Jim's.' En he made 'im git out meat, meal, 'lasses en sugar, en tole 'im t' take hit t' Jim's house en set it inside uv de do'. En, folkses, de nex' mo'nin' de rations all gone en de sack folded up en layin' right whar he leffit.

"Things rock along dissaway, dey did, all de yeah, Marster sen'in' Jim's rations eve'y Sa'day, en ev'y night he walk out t' de woodpile, en de jail, en de tree, en de cow lot, en de tree ag'in, en den he come in de house.

"Come Sa'day night 'fo' de las' Sunday in October, Marster tole Tom t' stay wid him t'night. En dey set in Marster's room jes lak dey done befo'. My daddy set in de chimbley cornder en de Marster-man rock in de big cheer en smoke 'is pipe en eve'y once in a w'ile he listen. Some'eres 'fo' midnight dat old scrich owul gi'n a holler en Marster jump up, he did, en say, 'Come on,' en out dey went, dey did, Marster in front en Tom foll'in' sorta slow. 'Fo' he cotch up wid 'im, he seed 'im git up off'n 'is knees by de tree en come meetin' 'im, en he say, 'Dey wet, dey wet.' An' he hilt out 'is han's jes lak he done befo' en teched all uv 'is fingers wid 'is thumbs. En when dey got t' de light, 'is han's wuz all bloody jes lak dey wuz befo'. Den dey prayed—didn' try t' wash 'em 'ca'se dey knowed 'twouldn' do no good; but my daddy say dey sho prayed manful! Twoge de las' de Marster say, 'How long, Lawd, mus' Ah suffer? Have mussey Jesus fer jes a li'l w'ile.' Den he gin a long bref, he did, en stood up en said, quick-lak, 'Thank you, Jesus, fer dat.' En w'en dey look at 'is han's de blood wuz gone. Marster fell on de bed, he did, en right off he wuz sno'in'. W'en he look out de winder, daddy see day wuz breakin'. Dey had prayed all night ag'in!

"De nex' yeah, en de nex', en de nex', dey wa'n't no change. Marster kep' a-walkin' eve'y night en lookin' fer sump'm, en eve'y Sa'day 'fo' de las' Sunday in October he git 'is han's bloody at de foot uv de tree, en him en ole Tom, my daddy, pray hit off. No, dey wa'n't no change cep'm Marster—whut nuse to be a sprightly youngish sorta man—got walkin' stooped over en slow, en 'is face got wrinkled, en 'is haid turn w'ite— plum' w'ite. En all de time he walkin' roun' he talkin to his- se'f en singing', but cain't nobody un'erstan' whut he sayin', en de folkses all say hit's Jim talkin' er ilse he talkin' t' Jim.

"Well, de Sa'day come w'en Jim been daid fi' yeahs, en de Marster-man wuz gi'in' out rations, en at de las' he say, 'Whar Jim's sack en all?' En ain' nobody seed it. Den he tole one uv de udder mens t' run git it. En he did run, en fas' too, 'ca'se de sun wuz mos' down, en he knowed de bes' place fer him t' be wuz away f'um dar. W'en he come back he say, 'Dem las' week rations dar yit. Dey ain' been teched.' En Marster ast 'im wuz he sho, en he say, 'Yes suh, Marster, en ef you don' b'lieve me, you sen' anudder nigger en le' him see.' En Marster look at 'im sorta funny-lak, 'ca'se he knowed he's skeered, en he said, 'Nemmine,' he'd go hisse'f. W'en he come back, he wuz steppin' bris', lak he nuseter, en snappin' 'is fingers eve'y udder step. En he say, 'Dat's all, boys, en good night t' y'all,' en he smile *sho nuff* fer de fus' time sence hit happen. My daddy say he stayed wid 'im aw'ile en den ax 'im ef he wan' im' t' come back right atter supper. En he say he need'n come t'night, but jes sharp'm 'is razor fer 'im, 'ca'se he gwi shave t'night 'nstid uv in de mo'nin'. En w'en de razor sharp'm dey talk a w'ile, en my daddy say he ax 'im ag'in ef he wan' 'im t' stay. En he smile sorta quiet-lak, he did, en he say, 'Not t'night, Ole Nigger, not t'night.' En w'en he started t' leave 'im he tap 'im light on de shoulder en say, 'Don' know how Ah could git along widout you, Tom,' en den he shet de do'.

"Dat night my daddy say he couldn' sleep none 'ca'se w'en he comin' home he seed a big, black, yaller-eyed cat foll'in' 'im, en eve'y time he shet 'is eyes atter he lay down dat ole cat 'Me-yow!' outside de do', en he know hits a witch waitin' fer a chance t' ride 'im. He knowed how t' fix dat, he did; so he sprinkle a han'ful uv salt on de flo' en laid de broom (saige-grass, hit wuz, en dat's de bes') 'cross de do' so she couldn' git in. Once, w'ile he settin' by de fiah, he thought he hyeah Marster callin' 'im, en he started fer t' go, but w'en he tech de do' dat ole cat 'Me-yow' ag'in, en he know hit 'uz de witch whut call 'im, en ef he had a open dat do' she'd a got 'im, sho.

"De nex' mo'nin' a li'l 'fo' day de dogs in de quarters quit howlin' en de owuls quit shiverin'; dey'd been gwine on muchly all night. Daddy been lis'nin' hard all de night en ain' hyeahd nothin' but dat once w'en de witch call 'im, en now he crack de winder, he did, en look twoge de big house, an', fer de fus' time in five yeah, da' ain't no light burnin' in Marster's room. After day done broke good he went t' de house. En Marster's ole blue houn', whut wuz mighty ole now, he wuz, met 'im at de fron'chard gate, en 'is haid en tail wuz bofe droopin'. Wid narry word spoke atwix' 'em, dey bofe made fer de jail-house en 'fo' dey git dar, he seed sump'm, all crumple' up un'er de tree en 'is heart jump so high in 'is th'oat hit mos' choke 'im.

"Hit wuz de Marster-man, all dress up fit t' kill lak he gwine somewhar, but he had 'is razor in 'is han 'en one side uv 'is neck wuz cut mos' off. He been daid so long he stiff.

"F'um dat time on twel now, mos' any night w'en de signs right you kin see sump'm gwine f'um de woodpile t' de jail-house, en de tree, en de cow lot, en roun' de henhouse en back t' de tree, en hit's de Ole Marster-man, lookin' fer Jim. En jes once a yeah, on de Sa'day 'fo' de las' Sunday in October he fin' 'im. Fin' 'im at de foot uv de tree, en ef you stan'in' close you kin hyeah 'im say low-lak, 'He wet. He wet.' En den he say, 'Hit's blood. Hit's blood.' " Then in a tone entirely different from the one of dreadful monotony, Aunt Polly said, "Th'ow on a piece uv kindlin', Boy, de fiah's mos' out."

After the tension had passed, everybody tried to talk at once, and Aunt Polly was asked a number of questions, all of which she refused to answer. She was too good a story teller to cheapen the effect by answering questions or repeating any part of her tale.

"Nemmine now," she'd say, "dat's all fer t'night, 'sides dat, hit's gittin' late." This reminded Net that they had to get home, John did, anyway; so she said, "Well, goodnight, Ai'

Polly, us got t' go. Come on, Baby, le's go." But John shrank back with, "Don' le's go now, Net," and when she questioned him closely, and he said, "'Cause it dark out dar," she was much amused. "Lawd, Ai' Polly, ef he ain' skeered. Come on, Baby. Ah ai' gwi let nothin' hu'tchu." His faith in her prowess in worldly matters was boundless, but it didn't reach over into the world of "ha'nts"; so he still hesitated, held back, in fact, until Aunt Polly came to the rescue. She made one of the youngsters break a small branch from a peachtree that grew at her front door, and after studying it intently for a minute or so, she carefully selected three leaves, and spreading them on her lap, made her final selection by repeating some doggerel that was close kin to "Eeny, meeny, miny, mo." She ended with the three words, "Go, ha'nt, go," and she picked up the "go" leaf. Then from a tobacco sack hanging over the mantle-piece ("she'f," she called it), she took a "ghos' seed" and wrapped it in the leaf.

"Now heah, Honey," she said, "you hol' dis in yo' right han' tight twel you git home en don' be skeered. Long as you got dis in yo' han' dey ain't no sperrit whut ever lived kin come anywhar nigh you. Listen now. W'en you git home, jes ez you step up on de steps, th'ow hit over yo' lef' shoulder—*lef'*, mind you now—*lef'*. En don' look back twel you tech de do' facin'. Atter dat you be aw right, 'en you'll see dey ain' nothin' gwi hu'tchu. En t'morrow you kin git me anudder chaw uv 'bac'er. Hyeah?"

Due to Aunt Polly's charm, doubtless, nothing did hurt John on the way home, and next day she got the "bac'er."

THE TREE CASTS
SHADOWS

MATTISES

In the garden one spring morning, John undertook to correct Aunt Betsey's pronunciation. He was between twelve and thirteen then. School and the folks at home had improved his own pronunciation to some extent. He spoke fairly good English until he was excited, and then he forgot. Now he wanted to pass his knowledge along.

"Ai' Betsey," said he, "you mustn't say 'mattises,' it's 'to-ma-toes.' "

"Whut dat chu say?"

"There is no such thing as 'mattises,' Ai' Betsey. It's 'to-ma-toes.' "

"Now, bless Gawd! Do you hyeah dat chile, folkses?" She was talking to an imaginary audience, for no one else was around. "Jes listen t' 'im, folkses, please! *Jes* listen! 'Pears lak t' me dat hit wuz jes day 'fo' yistiddy he wuz bawn, en now hyere he tryin' t' tell de ole folks sump'm." Her disgust was indescribable. "J-e-s b-a-w-n, en tryin' t' tell de ole folks

144

sump'm; tryin' t' tell his granny, whut got chillun whut *got grown* chillun, dat mattises ain't mattises no mo', naw, dey is 'ter—m-a-r—ters.' Now, Honey, you listen t' me: 'Fo' you wuz bawn dey wuz mattises; dey wuz mattises back in Ferginny; dey been mattises right hyere twel now, en dey still is mattises. Don'chu be gwine roun' showin' yo' ignunce lak dat, Honey, en, 'bove all, don'chu n-e-v-u-h try t' tell de ole folks nothin'. Dey knows, Honey, better'n whut chu do."

She started to the house; and until she was out of sight John could hear her disgusted "Umph! Umph! Umph!" almost at every step. "Umph! Umph! Umph! Chillun tryin' t' tell ole folks mattises ain't mattises, dey is *ter-mar-ters!* Um gwi tell Ole Mis'."

In a little while Ole Mis' wanted to know what John had been doing to Betsey.

"Nothin' a-tall, Gran'ma," he said defensively, his English beginning to lapse. "I was jus' tellin' her how to say 'tomatoes' right."

"Lawsey me! sonny, was that all?" she laughed. "Betsey came to me all sputtering and saying, 'Young chillun ain't got no 'spec' fer whut ole folks know,' and left me under the impression that you had treated her disrespectfully. Grandma didn't think you had done that intentionally, and I am glad to know the trouble is no greater than that. But, Johnny, you have hurt your old Aunt Betsey's feelings, and I am sure you didn't want to do that, did you?"

"Why, no'm, Gran'ma, no'm! I wuz jus' tellin' her—"

"I know, Johnny," interrupted his grandmother, "and I feel sure you didn't mean to, but you *have* hurt her feelings, and now the thing for you to do is to 'unhurt' them, son. Go and do something for her."

"I don't know what to do, Gran'ma."

"Well, think it over, sonny, and do a little something for her. And remember this: Before you do any more correcting around here, you had better look after your own pronunciation; for, Johnny, it needs it."

After a time of deep thought, a bright idea struck John. He went to the garden, where he cut and trimmed two peachtree toothbrushes. Then he carried them to her.

"Look here, Ai' Betsey, whut I got you!"

"Now, bless Gawd! See whut dat chile done fotch 'is ole mammy? En peachtree, chillun! Ah been wantin' one fer de longes'." She had only to step outside her kitchen door to get one. "Bless 'is heart, he knows Ah laks 'em bitter."

Thus, all feeling of resentment was blown away. And that afternoon John heard Aunt Betsey saying to Aunt Nervy, "Sis Nervy, you jes don' know whut a good chile dat boy is. He jes lak his mammy when she 'uz little; en, ef me en Ole Mis' kin keep 'im hyere wid us, he gwi grow up dat way; us'll see t' dat."

TIAH'D

Aunt Betsey was failing. Little bursts of momentary impatience, scarcely noticed at first, finally developed into violent fits of temper. Anything or nothing would throw her into a spell, and the awestruck servants watched her fearfully while she was in one of these tantrums; for in some way she had convinced the negroes that throwing a "kittle" full of hot water on them was the mildest thing she could do.

Mars John laughed at this, but the fiat went forth: "Let Betsey alone; she's not well. That's what's the matter."

After one of her outbursts they called in John from hunting wasps' nests and told him Aunt Betsey was sick; might be dying; to get the doctor, quick! John jumped on his pony and went lickety-split for the doctor, who lived six miles away. He was sitting on his porch, and when John rode up, he asked, "Well, young man, you seem to be in a hurry. Is anything wrong up your way?"

"Yes sir. Want you to come to see Ai' Betsey quick. She dying."

"Then there is no earthly use in my going if she is dying. Surely she is dead by now."

"Naw, she ain't, doctor," John insisted. "You come on!"

So the doctor caught up his horse and away they went. When they got to the yard gate, right by Aunt Betsey's house, who should come out to open it but Aunt Betsey herself!

"Howdy, Mars Joe," she greeted him happily, "how you do? Um sho is glad t' see you lookin' so well."

Doctor Joe looked at her in astonishment. "Why, Betsey," he said, "I thought you were dying!"

"Well, Mars Joe," she said, her voice suddenly weak as she pointed to her "chis," "Ah is mighty sick."

Doctor Joe's visit was turned into a social chat, much to John's delight; for as a teller of stories, the doctor was almost without an equal.

Not long after this Aunt Betsey had another of her spells. This time the attack was especially severe. Something had gone wrong in the kitchen, and when she went to the wood-pile for stove wood, John saw her drop to her knees, lift her hands to the heavens and almost scream, "How long, Lawd, how long? Lawd, whut *is* Ah done?" Then, bursting into tears, the first he had ever seen her shed, she ran into her house.

John told his Aunt, and she went immediately to see about it. Aunt Betsey was tossing and rolling and groaning on her bed. When she saw who was there, she quieted after a bit and Miss Sallie asked, "Mammy, what *is* the matter with you?"

"Um's jes tiah'd, Miss Sallie, Ah wants t' go t' live wid my chillun."

"Of course you may go, Mammy," Miss Sallie told her. "I'll send you in the morning."

The tears dried up and were not seen again. Aunt Betsey didn't cook any more that day, but next morning, bright and early, she was in the kitchen and had breakfast "in no time."

After a while, John, who was watching in sorrow, saw a wagon drive up to her door. Abe, the driver, said, "Ai' Betsey, us is ready fer you."

"Fer me? Fer whut?"

"Us gwi move you. Gwine take yo' things up home."

"You's gwine take nothin' f'um dis place but yo'se'f en dat waggin' 'way f'um my do'. Whut Ah wan' t' go dar fer w'en dat house already overrun wid chillun? En 'sides dat, 'sides dat, who gwine cook Mars John's en Miss Sallie's en Ole Mis's vittles ef Ah do go dar? En Ah tell you right now, Ah ain' gwine ha' none uv dese hyere fiel' niggers a-messin' up my kitchen! Go on 'way f'um hyere, nigger, Ah got t' go out t' de gyarden en git some greens—hit's mos' time t' start dinner."

This was the last of her fits of temper. After that she was always amiable and sweet. She visited in the quarters very little now, preferring to spend her afternoons in her house, or to sit in the shade of the trees. Here, Aunt Nervy, who was beginning to show her own years, visited Aunt Betsey almost daily. Their favorite place to sit was in Aunt Betsey's garden in the shade of the little elm (John's name-tree, not so little now) that they together had planted nearly fourteen years before.

Aunt Betsey leaned back in her chair against the name-tree and rubbed her head against it almost caressingly. "Sis Nervy," she said, looking at the sky through the leaves above, "Gawd's signs don' nevuh fail, do dey?"

"Not ez Ah knows uv, Sis Betsey," she answered. "Ah ain' got de 'membrance uv seein' narry one uv his good, true, en sho signs failin' yit, en dat's de trufe. Whut 'uz you thinkin' 'bout?"

"Dis tree—hit's a good sign, ain't it? Fer a while hit look lak hit 'uz gwi grow straight up en not spread none. Ah didn' lak dat, 'ca'se a name-tree ought t' spread out en gi' a good shade en he'p you. Dat's whut dis'n's doin' now, en dat boy gwi be jes lak it, thank Gawd fer dat."

They talked of various things, and after a bit Aunt Nervy commenced to hum and pat her foot on the ground; and when Aunt Betsey asked what she was humming, she sang aloud:

"Ah nevuh shell fergit dat day,
When Jesus wash' my sins away,
Lawd, you ought t' been dar ten thousan' yeahs—
Drinkin' wine.
Drinkin' wine, drinkin' wine.
Lawd, you ought t' been dar ten thousan' yeahs—
Drinkin' wine.

Drinkin' wine, drinkin' wine.
Lawd, you ought t' been dar ten thousan' yeahs—
Drinkin' wine.

He gi'n me a ho'n en he tole me to blow,
He gi'n me de seed en he tole me to sow,
Lawd, you ought t' been dar ten thousan' yeahs—
Drinkin' wine.

'Ligion is jes lak a bloomin' rose,
Dat none but dem dat feels hit knows,
Lawd, you ought t' been dar ten thousan' yeahs—
Drinkin' wine."

Then they sang together, the chorus first:

"Where will Ah be when de fus' trumpet soun'?
Oh where will Ah be when hit soun'?
Hit soun' so loud twel hit wake up de daid,
Oh where will Ah be when it soun'?

Ole Moses live twel he got ole—where shell Ah be?
Buried in de mount'ins so Um tole—where shell Ah be?

Gawd showed Norah by de rainbow sign—where shell Ah
    be?
No mo' watter but de fiah nex' time—where shell Ah be?

Ah nevuh shell fergit dat day—where shell Ah be?
When Jesus wash my sins away—where shell Ah be?

Sunday mo'nin' bright en fair—where shell Ah be?
Go'n' to hitch on my wings en try de air—where shell Ah
    be?

One dey ez Ah wuz walkin' roun'—where shell Ah be?
De ellermints open en de love come down—where shell Ah
    be?"

They sang others, the two old women, weaving and rocking
from side to side in an ecstasy of enjoyment, and wound up
with:

> "Mos' done trab'lin' de rough rocky road,
> Mos' done trab'lin' de rough rocky road,
> Mos' done trab'lin' de rough rocky road,
> Go'n' to cah'y my soul to de Lawd.
>
> Boun' to cah'y my soul to Jesus,
> Boun' to cah'y my soul to Jesus,
> Boun' to cah'y my soul to Jesus,
> Boun' to cah'y my soul to de Lawd."

Suddenly, Aunt Betsey said, "Ah wants t' go home en res'."
"Ma'm?"

"Ah wants t' go home en lay down, Sis Nervy," she said,
smiling at Aunt Nervy's startled face, "Um's tiah'd."

"Lawd, Sis Betsey, Ah thought you wuz talkin' 'bout dat
udder home."

"Naw, Honey," she smiled at her, "Ah wa'n't thinkin' 'bout
dat; but dat home ain' so fur away, needer. 'Twon' be long
now; 'twon' be long 'fo' Um's 'walkin' t' Jerusalem jes lak
John,'" she said, quoting from one of the songs they had sung.

"Lawd, have mussey! Sis Betsey, don' talk lak dat," Aunt
Nervy begged. "You's good fer a long time yit."

"Mos' done trab'lin' de rough rocky road"

"Ah knows Um is, Sis Nervy—Gawd willin'; but dey ain't no tellin' how soon dat time gwi be."

They walked towards the house, slowly. At the garden gate, Aunt Betsey turned to look at the name-tree. "Fo'teen yeahs gone us planted dat tree, Sis Nervy," she said. "Fo'teen yeahs gone, de fus' uv dis yeah comin', us planted it; en, Lawd, Lawd, Lawd! how dey is growed—bofe uv'm!"

A little while later John was called to go for the doctor. Aunt Betsey was sick this time.

"Just a general breakdown," the doctor said. "She won't suffer, but there's nothing to do but hope."

Aunt Nervy and two other women stayed with her, and during the night she died.

Next morning, after John's first tears had dried, Aunt Nervy sought him out and led him toward Aunt Betsey's house.

"'Long 'bout midnight," Aunt Nervy said, "she ax me fer a drink uv watter, en when Ah got up t' git it, she say, 'Sis Nervy,' she say, 'Gawd's signs don' nevuh fails, does dey?' En Ah say, 'No'm,' en went t' de do' atter de watter. When Ah op'm it, a bright, bright stare fell. Hit mus' ha' been her stare Honey, 'ca'se, when Ah got back t' de bed, she wuz gone jes easy, lak dat—gone.

"Now you come on in hyere wid me. Ah wants t' show you sump'm."

John went with her into the house and stood by the bed as Aunt Nervy, with one hand on his shoulder, pulled the sheet from Aunt Betsey's face. He had thought of death, always, as a dreadful horror; but his shudder left him as he looked at the smile he saw there.

"Why, Aunt Nervy," he said in surprised wonder, "she's laughin'!"

"Dat's whut Ah wanted you t' see, Honey, see en 'member." After a little pause she continued softly, "Dyin' cain' be bad, Honey, kin it, ef you kin smile lak dat?"